I0742588

EYES OF AMBER

BY

ANYA STASSIY

CHAPTER 1

The air in the hospital parking garage was refreshingly cool: the June sun and humidity hadn't managed to penetrate the concrete walls of the building. It was forty minutes past seven in the evening and Leo had finally finished his third ER shift in a row. He was looking forward to the weekend, and to getting some much-needed rest. The garage was quiet—the new shift had already started and the staff of the previous one had already escaped into the evening. Only the distant screeching of brakes echoed, bouncing against the walls.

Leo recognized the gaunt figure pacing by his car. Seeing Laura again was unpleasant. He clenched his teeth, took a deep breath, and reminded himself to have patience...This woman was ill. She had lost control of her life a long time ago—years of hard drugs had withered her body away to a thin, unremarkable presence. Her young age of twenty-seven was hidden behind a wrinkled, pale face etched in scars and fresh sores. This woman's once blond hair was now jet black and close-shaven on the right side. The lopsided haircut reflected her out-of-balance nature.

"You have to stop; this is not healthy for you," he reprimanded the thin, anxious woman.

Leo had urged Laura to stop stalking him countless times, but she would merely disappear for a few days and then return again. He hadn't seen her in weeks, and hoped that this time she would finally leave him alone. He was disappointed to find her waiting in the hospital garage.

"Oh, now you care about my health?" she said as she nervously played with her fingers. "I have to behave like a psychotic, crazy woman for you to pay attention to me. How long has it been, huh? How long? Months, weeks since I was able to speak to you!" The nares of her reddened nose flared fast as she yelled.

Leo looked into his stalker's shining eyes, her pinpoint pupils barely visible.

"We discussed everything and I told you to stop contacting me," he said carefully, taking a step back. "I do not have feelings for you. I am not your physician. I do not want to resort to filing a harassment report, but you are not giving me any choice." he was growing angry with her, but tried to keep his voice calm. The concern for her well-being was evaporating; he just wanted her to stop obsessing over him.

"It is you who is not giving me any choice! All I wanted was just a little bit of your attention. I just wanted you to hear how I feel about you!" She stretched out her hand towards his face, but Leo quickly steered away from her reach. He was careful not to stand too close to this woman.

"Laura, I helped you when you were brought to the ER. You overdosed, and I was able to help you get better, but that's where our relationship ended. I was nice to you because I was behaving professionally." Leo paused, gauging her reaction. She stood in front of him, small and pitiful. Her gaze moved quickly between the mouth and eyes of the one who didn't want her attention. It was difficult for Leo to speak to her so harshly, but he decided to stand his ground. "I never had any feelings for you, and I still don't. Stop sending me gifts, stop waiting for me after work, and stop coming to the ER with made-up issues." The hands in his pockets were clenching into fists to steady the volume of his voice and emotions. "If you want me to, I can give you names of psychiatrists that can help you." He couldn't help but treat her as a patient…He saw that she was sick, and that it was her disease that was controlling her. However, his rational response hit a wall against the irrational mind of Laura.

"I don't fucking need any more psychiatrists! I am already seeing two. All they do is prescribe pills and more pills." Her voice grew louder, echoing in the emptiness of the garage.

"Then I have had enough. I have to go! I've had a long day at work." There was no point in saying anything else; he couldn't help her. Leo started to look for a way to escape this unpleasant encounter.

"I can make your day better. What do you need?" she paused, trying to catch Leo's gaze. "Dinner? Massage? We can just fuck…" She grabbed his arm, holding on tight. Her touch only irritated and angered Leo more. She started to sob; this tactic was all too familiar. His instinct would nudge him to comfort anyone who was crying, but such a gesture tonight would only feed Laura's mania. He towered over her, like an emotionless, impermeable wall, but she continued to try and conquer it. "I will do anything you want. Just let me love you."

All Leo wanted was for this woman to disappear and never bother him again with her attachment issues. A few months ago, she was just another patient—brought in together with Leo's brother, Danny. Both were found unresponsive in a car in the parking lot of the nearby mall. Simultaneous codes were run on both, but only Laura survived. His brother succumbed to the addiction that had plagued his mind and body for the past seven years.

Leo often thought that Danny had wanted to die. He was always trying the next drug...looking for the highest high that would keep him absent from reality the longest. On that night, he had reached the peak of his search, and his body had given up. Leo told Laura about Danny's death himself: she'd had no tears—they were just acquaintances that shared crack once in a while, so they could both watch out for each other in case of an overdose. Leo felt an obligation to try and encourage her to quit drugs—something that he'd failed to do for Danny. She finally broke down and promised to get clean, grateful for him saving her life. Once discharged, she did just that, and even found a job working in a pet shop. Three months later, she started sending fruit baskets, flowers, coffee, lunches; waiting for him to leave the hospital and inviting him to have dinner with her. Those small gestures quickly escalated to ER visits with abdominal pain, headaches, and unexplained itching. Leo recognized that Laura had escaped one addiction and plunged herself into another: one where he was the drug. He hated and despised her for it. The weight of his failure to help this patient doubled the grief for the loss of his brother.

"No. There will never be anything between us. I have to go." He jerked his arm and broke the tight grip she had on his sleeve. In a few quick steps, Leo reached his vehicle. He hoped that his car would start on a first try. The turn of the keys and the gentle pressure on the gas pedal made the engine rumble and a sigh of relief escaped his chest. He pressed the gas pedal to the floor sending the tires spinning, filling the garage with smoke and obscuring Laura. Leo might have to file that police report, and apply for a protective order against her.

He wondered if this woman's behavior was the Karma for all the women he'd hurt in the past. All he used to care about was the physical satisfaction of catching his prey, only to leave it behind for the next chase. No woman ever challenged him emotionally or intellectually—maybe it was him getting closer to the age of thirty, or maybe it was the loss of his brother, but satisfying his physical desire was no longer enough. He wanted to find the one who would want him to stay; he wanted a relationship filled with happiness. He was thinking about the future and he wanted to be content.

CHAPTER 2

Phweeeeeet! The sound of the boiling kettle is getting louder, so I hurry into the kitchen to start my evening tea routine. I cozy up on my chair and kick my feet up on the ottoman, ready to indulge in a piece of dark chocolate as I slurp hot tea with milk. My anticipation of a moment of bliss is rudely interrupted by the doorbell.

I open the door to a singing tornado of elegantly dressed, perfectly made up and manicured woman that is my mother. "Hello, darling!" she thrills, rushing into my apartment. "How are you?" she asks as she gives me a soft kiss and a hug. "Are you alone?" Her R's are punctuated rolls, highlighting an accent that gives away her Russian descent.

"Of course I am alone, Mama. Come in. Do you want a cup of tea?" I ask, but secretly hope she will say no so that I don't have to share my chocolate. My mother has a habit of stopping by unannounced. She doesn't believe me when I tell her that I am just watching TV, or just reading a book, or just doing nothing, and that I am just doing all those things by myself. She hopes to catch me with a secret boyfriend: one that I wouldn't want to introduce her to for some unknown reason.

"Thank you, Angel," she says in her crisp singing voice, loud enough to make her entrance known in case there is anyone else besides me in the apartment. When she doesn't hear a response from a secret boyfriend, she neatly takes off her high heels and puts pink slippers on, the ones reserved just for her. "But your father and I are going out. He is downstairs trying to find a parking spot."

She shimmies behind me as we go into the living room and sits on the couch. I sit down beside her, brushing off invisible crumbs between us as I quickly glance through the room to make sure it is somewhat orderly, and I don't have a bra hanging somewhere in the open. I breathe a sigh of relief when my scan reveals no major housekeeping disaster. My independent living frequently brings on a roll of the eyes and a sigh of hopelessness at my solo existence.

She shifts to the edge of the couch with her back perfectly straight, her manicured hands placed over her lap. I sink deeper and put my feet up and then down, knowing that my mother will not approve of bare feet on the furniture. She stays unusually quiet until I notice a smirk like that of a mischievous kid who has done something so exciting she is about to burst from anticipation. The only thing that is stopping the explosion is the possibility of a rebuke from a stern parent. She stares at me with a grin, welcoming my questioning.

"Yeees?" I stretch it purposefully, hoping to slow down the flood that is about to pour out of my mother.

"So, a couple of days ago, I met my girlfriends for lunch. It was me, Lisa, Gloria, Aunt Libby and Anna. Do you remember Bella—Bella Kogan, and her sister?"

"Mghm," I nod, vaguely recognizing the names.

"Well, anyway...We used to work together in the museum. So, Anna, who is Bella's sister, she has a son. Max—his name is Max—is thirty, and a lawyer. He has never been married. He's handsome...I made sure I looked at his picture." She winks at me, justifying her evaluation of his attractiveness, "And so I gave Anna your number so that Max can give you a call!" She tries to rapid fire the information, before I tune her out. She claps her hands: she is her own cheerleader.

I get up and put down my now lukewarm tea on the TV stand, knowing that an evening of bliss is ruined and will instead be spent in self-pity. My mom's failure to catch me with a secret boyfriend continues to feed her passion for setting me up with a real boyfriend. She is tenacious; she feels it is her duty to find a match for me, since as she puts it: "You, my darling, are for some reason not interested in creating your own happy ending. I don't understand your generation. All you do is either study or work; no one is interested in finding love. There is no romance. To find it, you have to put some effort into it. No little computer game or whatever it is called will find your true love, and don't roll your eyes at me, missy—you know I am right!" She wags her finger to scold me for grimacing at her lecture. "Everyone is just staring at the phones all the time. They are not looking at each other. You need to see the person...smell them, touch them, laugh with them, talk to them. You youngsters don't even know how to write!

All you do is send some mumbo jumbo and yellow faces to each other."

"They are not 'yellow faces'. Well, I guess they are… But they are called emojis, and the mumbo jumbo is an abbreviation for a phrase—to make it easier to type; like, 'lol', which actually means laughing out loud." I calmly explain all of this to my mom, who is unfamiliar and purposefully disregarding modern conversational language. I have learned over the years that arguing with her while she is delivering her 'life lesson lectures' is completely useless. It is always better to weather the storm of her words quietly, and almost still.

"And I personally think that romance has died. When the Internet was created, there became no need for it anymore. People are more straightforward: they don't want to waste time wooing someone. You are either the right candidate, or you are not." I lay out my logic for her.

"Are you talking about love, my dear? And you use such terms as a 'candidate'? This is not a corporate job interview…We are talking about feelings here. And yes, wooing is absolutely important. It creates a mystery, and with it, the anticipation, and the butterflies. All I know is that there is no shortcut to happiness."

"Mama, I don't want to meet anyone—not online, and not in real life. I don't want to be set up with anyone. I just want to be by myself." I get up from the couch and walk to the window with my back turned to my mother. "I don't need anyone to fulfill me or be my other half: I am enough, just as I am—by myself, and for myself!" The annoyance in my voice slows down her rush of information to a careful treading.

"Honey," she walks up to me, takes my hand into hers and gently pulls me to face her. I oblige and turn towards her. A timid smile graces the beautiful face of my mother; her eyes are smart twinkles that look at me patiently. She keeps a hold of my hand and with the other, tucks a loose strand of hair behind my ear. Her hand gives me a soft, reassuring squeeze, and she queries endearingly: "You know I love you? I just want you to be happy. There is someone out there for you. And I just want to help things along," she says apologetically. She changes her strategy now; the pushy lecturing subsides, and she gives me a chance to talk.

"I know, Mama—thanks, but it doesn't mean you have to set me up with every available guy. I just finished medical school. I am about to start the residency, and I don't have time for dating right now!"

"When you were in high school, you were not interested in boys, and I was happy about it. In college, you were consumed with excelling in pre-med. In medical school, you were too busy becoming the best physician and now you are finally done, and you are still too busy. And so now, I worry. You are my only child, Mila. Dad and I are not getting any younger. We want to see you settled; we want to enjoy grandchildren." My mother turns up the guilt setting, and I know I am losing the battle. I decide to change my tone—before she turns on the waterworks—and before I will feel like I have to agree to anything she asks.

"I am sure l will feel it, but at the right time, with the right guy." I pause, doubting my own confidence. "*Maybe* I will feel it...I just don't want to force anything. I don't want it to be another job. I work hard enough for everything else: I don't want to fight for a chance—a mere possibility of meeting someone that I can coexist with until I am old. Plus, I think the idea of love is a made-up fairytale that really doesn't exist." I finish with a sigh of poorly hidden frustration.

"Is that what you think of mine and Dad's marriage? That we are just 'coexisting' until we shrivel up and die of old age?" My mother's eyes swell with tears.

"Of course not, Mama! You and Papa are different." I rush to give my reassurance so the tears don't start to flow.

"We are no different than any other couple who was open to love, and believed in it," my mother says softly.

"I just don't believe that you can feel...feel something for a person you don't really know and may never truly know. It is so unexplainable to me. I can't rely just on feelings; what I can rely on is my knowledge, and my knowledge tells me that all this supposed feeling of love is nothing but a series of chemical reactions." I try to escape the gentle but firm grasp of my mother's hand who stares at me in disbelief, as if hearing of my persuasion for the first time.

"Honey, you are no exception. You will find the right one, and when you do, you will feel...not some chemical reaction...but a pull of desire to be with the person because it feels good, not because it is convenient. Despite all the fights and differences, you still want to be next to him until the end. He will be making you a better person as he will strive to be a better one himself. Those are the true love stories."

"Mama, you are such a romantic. I don't think I inherited that gene from you."

"I am making it happen for you, honey. All you have to do is show up." She stares, almost without blinking, into my eyes, still expecting me to agree to follow through with her set up.

I roll my eyes as I breathe out. "OK Mama; I will go." Since my grandmother died six months ago, I cannot refuse my mom's requests, no matter how ridiculous they may be. Her face lights up with a satisfied smile and she gives me a quick peck on the cheek.

"That's my girl! You never know...He might be your Arthur Grey!" She almost sings joyfully. "I will make sure Anna gives him your phone number," she says under her breath and nods as if giving herself a mental check mark for another accomplishment. She tilts her head slightly to the side, looking somewhere into the distance.

"Mama? Hello there..." I try to bring her back. "Paging Moon from Earth...Are you still with me?"

"Of course; I am right here. I am just thinking," she giggles mischievously and pats my cheek.

"Mama, you know that Scarlet Sails is just a fairy tale?" I remind her.

"But fairy tales do exist. You just have to believe in them, and recognize them when they are right in front of you!" she says to me, unbothered by my attack on her unwavering belief in made-up love stories.

"One more thing...Here—I brought you the box of grandma's things. I finally got around to cleaning out her room; I know that she wanted you to have this.

She had a special connection with you that I never did. I think she saw a lot of herself in you. From the moment you were born, she would say, "This angel is special.""

I glance at the simple wooden box, and the smell of rose water—so often worn by my grandma—hits my nose as if she were right next to me. Her absence still seems unreal. The size of her personality, now gone from my life, leaves an unfillable void that chokes me to tears every time I think of her. I take a deep breath and quickly brush away a free-falling tear before my mother can see it.

My mother took grandma's death hard; she still cries every day. A sappy commercial can trigger the crying, as can an elderly lady walking on the street, and even a glimpse of grandma's belongings. I can't even imagine the flood of tears that accompanied the clearing of her room.

"You should have called me. I would have helped you."

"No, no," Mama straightens herself out. "I needed to do it; to at least start…at my own pace. I needed to go through my thoughts, and grieve. There are letters in there between your grandmother and her fiancé. I believe she never told you this story, but she was to be married… Then, World War II started, and her fiancé disappeared in the battlefield. She saved the letters that they wrote to each other during that period. At one point, she was thinking of writing a book about her experience and I translated those letters and typed them up. It ended up being too painful of a memory for Grandma, and we have done nothing further with them."

"Were you OK reading about Grandma's other love before she was married, and had you?"

"Sure. I know she loved my father and I am not naive to believe that my mother, who married Grandpa at thirty years of age, had no other relationships. I think the love for the man in the letters saved her life while she was in the besieged Leningrad; she wouldn't have survived if she hadn't believed that there was someone waiting for her."

"What do you want me to do with them?"

"Read them. They might teach you something you didn't know about your grandmother. They are a piece of history. Your grandmother's generation lived through the horrific tragedy of war; we shouldn't forget that."

My father quietly walks into the living room; he has finally found a parking spot. His presence interrupts our little moment of grieving and of remembering the woman who was so dear to all of us.

"Ah! My two favorite girls!" He rumbles as he stretches out his arms, welcoming a hug from both of us. His arms are long and large, with callus covered fingers from the years of boxing he did in his youth. He has recently started to grow out a beard, which is surprisingly bushy, and he's shaved his head due to the lack of hair growing on it.

"Why are you two so gloomy?" He gives me a quick wink and gently lifts my chin to place a kiss on my forehead. I smile softly, appreciating his presence and understanding. I nuzzle into his wide chest and I see my mother lovingly smack him for intruding on her business. I squeeze my dad tight and feel a squeeze back in return. His hug always makes me feel better—

protected. I breathe in a familiar scent of a cologne that hasn't changed in years, and enjoy a brief moment of complete calm.

"Honey, I have to steal your mother away now, but you have to promise that you will come out with us next time. You are turning into a recluse. And you are too beautiful to hide behind all these walls." As he says it, he puts a finger under my chin and raises it up; it makes me feel that I am still a child. His kind blue eyes, the same color as mine, pierce me, always letting me know that I am the center of his universe.

"All right, Dad. Next time, I promise I will go out with you." I commit to the outing before he releases me from his hug. With his other arm still around my mother's shoulder, my father leads her into the hallway where he lets my mom slip into her high heels, and passes her handbag to her. I lean on the wall, observing their seamless movement to a melody known only to couples who are meant for each other.

My mother softly presses her hand against my cheek, then smiles as she leans and places a soft kiss on the other cheek.

"Bye, darling! I will call you tomorrow! And I think you do have the love gene. It is just…How do you say it in your medical terms? Ah! It hasn't been *activated* yet!" she says with a twinkle of mischief in her eyes burning bright.

"OK, Mama." I breathe out with a sigh, knowing that there will be no escape from a barrage of questions regarding Max, who she will ensure calls me by the end of tomorrow.

"Bye, honey!" says my dad, as he envelopes me in another one of his bear-like hugs and squeezes me, lifting me for a brief moment from the floor. I squeal with excitement, cherishing this moment of tenderness. I close the door behind my parents, who walk off hand in hand, my mom leaning her head on my father's shoulder. Witnessing the ease of their affection releases the nag of loneliness, and the realization that I do long for affection; however, I quickly shoo it away, telling myself that being single is truly best for me.

• • •

I shuffle back to my living room with my grandmother's wooden box in hand, and sink into the couch. I now put my feet up, and leave them there. I open the cover slowly, not knowing what the contents of the box behold—besides the letters that my mother mentioned. Right at the top of the box is a picture of me, about two years old, in the arms of my grandmother. The black and white photo, now more yellow and grey with curling edges, radiates pure happiness; both of us are laughing at something, looking straight at each other, forehead to forehead. Another picture is of a younger grandma: the date on the back is June 1939; she would have been seventeen at the time. Standing in the tall grass, a knee-length summer dress drapes her thin, teenage figure. She has long, red curly hair just like me. "We have been kissed by the sun," she used to tell me when I complained that the kids teased me, calling me a "carrot top". My grandma looks so happy and carefree—not knowing of the hardship that she would need to endure in her near future.

The next picture is of my grandmother and my grandfather on their wedding day. She looks so regal in a lace dress and a veil draping to the floor. Both of them, as was the norm, are not smiling in this official wedding picture, but knowing both of them, they were laughing right after the picture was taken. My grandfather was the biggest jokester; he proclaimed his purpose in life was to make my grandmother laugh all the time. My grandmother often said that she married him because he knew how to make her smile.

The box also contains some jewelry made of amber, my grandma's favorite stone, that she frequently wore. At the bottom of the box, I find a folder tucked into a leather-bound book. When I open the book, it turns out to be a journal with some pages ripped out, and the others bearing no handwriting. The folder contains sheets of typed up translations of the letters; to each sheet is attached the original handwritten letter. I recognize my grandmother's handwriting right away— it is a neat cursive with round, curvaceous letters. The ink on the originals has started to fade and the paper looks too fragile to be unfolded, which I decide not to do, since I can't read Russian anyway. I examine each letter on the outside. The letters written by my grandmother are the pages torn from the diary, and the letters received from the battlefront—now yellow, stained and folded into triangles—have the address written right on them, since no envelopes were used at that time.

I look at the dates of the letters, which are already in chronological order with the earliest letters at the top. I wonder what I will discover in these letters... Why did my grandmother keep them all this time?

25 May, 1941

My sunny Iskra,

I cannot believe that we are to be together soon. Finally, my studies in medical school are over and I will be joining you in Leningrad. We are most certainly going to enjoy a few weeks together before we go to Odessa to become man and wife and start a life as a proper couple. Can we go to your aunt Olya's dacha in Priutino? Will she not mind a lanky spectacled man intruding on her gardening kingdom?

I miss the vastness of the fields and the smell of the forest in the early morning. We can spend days by the lake and nights in the softness of the grass just staring at the stars wondering what they hold for us. I can finally hold you, caress your body, breathe in the smell of your skin and touch the softness of your fiery red hair.

I have already arranged for us a room where we will be able to have Dar with us. I miss that grumpy, lazy dog. My mother is sending you her love. Our wedding has her running all over the town in preparation. I think she has mistaken me for a bride and collected quite a "dowry" of goose feather pillows and comforters; she has also invited half of the neighborhood to celebrate our marriage.

I cannot wait for our life to begin! I am eagerly looking forward to seeing you.

P.S. I have been so elated that I have completely forgotten to ask about your semester. I bring my apologies for being so selfishly absorbed with my euphoria. I have no doubt, that the most beautiful woman will become the smartest botanist of our country and will successfully pass her exams.

I kiss your gentle hands and wait in agony for us to be together.

~

10 June, 1941

My Dear Jacob,

The last letter from you has given me the most joy. I am glad to find that you are in such high spirits about our upcoming wedding. I must say that I would rather avoid a large celebration. I think it takes away from the intimate moment of two people joining their lives together, but of course, I love your mother too much to deprive her of such a celebration.

Thank you for being the most supportive about my studies. I must remind you that my career as a botanist will end with me teaching biology in one of the schools. There is gossip of increased questioning and screenings by NKVD. People are whispering about the war with Germany; they are hushed quickly with the loud proclamation that Hitler will not dare to break the peace pact.

I have two finals left and then aunt Olya and I will leave for Priutino. We will anxiously wait for you there, my love. Aunt Olya is eager to put you to work on her sauna and she has a few more projects for you to occupy your time. I promise I will steal you away so we can enjoy the forest and the lake. Please telegraph me your date and time of arrival. Kissing your beautiful eyes and waiting to rest my head on your chest. Yours forever, loving Iskra.

I decide to stop my peering into the past life of these two people, and let the evening escape as I digest the small history trip that I was being taken on via this correspondence. My chocolate stays uneaten and a cold cup of tea is moved to the sink as I ready to go to bed, hoping for a restful night. I close my eyes and smile, remembering the nights when my mother would tell me yet one more time of a girl named 'Assol' who was foretold that her soulmate would come for her under the scarlet sails. She never gave up until Arthur Grey fulfilled the premonition, and they lived happily ever after.

CHAPTER 3

My parents met when both of them were eighteen years of age. Both children of Russian immigrants, they were introduced when their parents met up with more friends who had escaped Soviet Russia, seeking better lives in America. My father loves to tell the story of how they met. His recollection of the moments of that chance encounter were always accompanied by a big smile that never seemed to leave his face.

"We had been in the States for two weeks. I had just turned eighteen upon our arrival. I spoke very little of broken English, but I tried my best—we wanted to be Americans after all. We were constantly meeting some distant cousins, aunts, uncles, and friends of the family. My parents were able to get a one bedroom apartment on Brighton Beach. The place was small. The outside windows faced the train tracks and the whole building shook when a train went by. We didn't know what we would do: where to go to buy groceries, where to get medicine, or how to find a job. But we were the happiest of people: we had made it to America. On one of the warm evenings, some friends of my parents invited us out to the boardwalk to catch up—so they could hear how bad we had it, and for them to tell us how good everything had turned out for them. I didn't particularly want to go, but it was a hot evening, and I had nothing to do, so I trailed behind my parents onto the boardwalk. When I reached the top of the ramp, something made me look up: there, by the banister, I saw her. She was a vision." Then my father would always look into the distance as though having déjà vu of that first image of my mother.

"She had a light blue dress that draped over her figure, a long, thick braid down to her waist, and fine wisps of hair were blowing like a veil over her face. She was clasping her wrist with her right hand and gazing sadly into the sunset. When I saw that gaze, I knew I would do anything to see her smile. She, of course, turned out to be the daughter of the friends that we were meeting. I don't think I struck her as a prince charming when she shook my hand hello…" This line was always accompanied by the loudest of belly laughs, "…but I made her smile. And you know how I did it?" not waiting to hear our memorized response, he would continue to tell the story as if for the first time.

"Our parents stayed on the boardwalk, but we took our shoes off and went closer to the water. There, acting as a perfect gentleman, I put my jacket down on the sand for your mom to sit on. She continued to sadly look into the horizon. I found a shell, a perfectly ordinary shell. As I gifted it to her I said, 'This is a happy shell; the one who possesses it never feels sadness or grief. I will honor you with this gift if you promise to treasure it.' I tried to sound very important and serious to make it believable. Your mother took it, pressed it to her heart and gave me the biggest smile that I have ever seen.

'I promise,' she said. For the next two weeks, we were inseparable. By the end of the two weeks, I told her she would be my wife." At the end of this story my dad would always stretch out his feet, put both hands behind his head, sigh, and drift back into that moment in time, where the smile that my mother gave him was his biggest accomplishment.

That shell occupied a prominent place in a shadow box on the shelf amongst the treasured literary classics. My mother also placed their wedding picture and a handwritten note saying, '*Forever Happy*' inside of the box as a reminder of the promise she made on that day.

I don't think I have ever seen them argue. They never had a screaming, in your face, offensive, slamming doors kind of a fight. They bickered over small things, but those insignificant quarrels passed without leaving any footprint on their significant relationship. I still catch them stealing a quick kiss when we watch a movie, and I see them snuggling in the reflection of the TV screen. My parents preserve their love by never texting; they call instead, and they always say I love you at the end of the phone call to each other. They leave each other little notes around the house. I once found a yellow sticky note inside the coffee jar intended for my father. My mother had drawn a smiley face with a slight smirk and under it she wrote, "Have a wonderful day! Don't forget to kiss me! And don't forget I love you!" And so, my parents' behavior set an incredible standard for my own love life.

No one could ever measure up; none lasted past a few dates. My straightforward approach to weeding out unbefitting candidates eliminated even the most stoic and persistent ones. I was searching for a feeling, a feeling that I myself had never experienced, but felt that I needed to have for my "happily ever after". I wanted to feel that there was nothing that could separate us. That *we* were strong: supportive of each other, protective of each other—that we could do anything together. That notion of '*us*' that I was searching for always missed the mark, or maybe it was me who lacked something. The guy was either too concerned about his school or work and not enough about me, or I was too concerned about my career path, and not the needs of the guy. I had planned a trip of a lifetime plus all the pit stops, but I couldn't find the one I would want to go with on the trip. I never got "the feeling" from anyone.

My grandmother was my guide from an early age. She enjoyed instilling in me life lessons about love and happiness, and used to tell me how I had a special spark; I just needed to find the right person to spend my life with. If I made a mistake in my selection, one of two things would happen: my spark would go out, or my significant other would burn in the light of my personality. And so, her teachings added another layer of pressure to my search criteria.

By the time I had decided to go to medical school, any possibility of romance had faded. Everyone around me thought only of their grades, the next test, the next paper, and maybe an extra half an hour of sleep. So, the last relationship unraveled before I could even call it a relationship, and the dating stopped completely. I lived vicariously through my roommate, Michelle, who was already working as a Physician Assistant, and was enjoying the single life—the dinner dates; the one night stands.

I was living a lonely life, and if it were not for my mother's cooking I would have been surviving off of only coffee, instant oatmeal, instant noodles, and take out.

CHAPTER 4

Next morning, I am rudely awakened by my cell phone. It takes me a few seconds to find it in my half-asleep state. I pick it up after accidentally knocking it off the nightstand, and in my attempt to grab it, I fall out of bed myself.

"He-Hello?" I stutter, trying to rub away sleep from my eyes. But all I hear is background conversation that I can't make out.

"Hello?! Is anybody there?" I question without hidden exasperation.

"Mila—good morning! This is the secretary for Max Kogan. Your mother gave him your number." Her voice is crisp, deep, and business like.

How my mother manages to accomplish everything in the shortest amount of time is still a secret to me. "Hi! How are you?" I mutter, thinking of what to say next.

"I am fine, thank you for asking. Max is on a conference call all morning, but he is free for lunch. Can you meet him around one-thirty? Would a sushi place work for you?"

"Sure, sushi would work."

"OK, one-thirty then. I will text you the address of the place. Have a pleasant day!" She hangs up and I feel as though I have just been summoned to an important meeting that I cannot fail to attend. I stare at the phone for a few seconds, still lying on the floor. I jump at the *ping* of a new text message that contains the address for meeting Max. I blow a loose strand of hair from my face. A gut feeling tells me that it is not a good sign that Max didn't call himself, but instead tasked his secretary with organizing his personal matters.

I glance at the clock. Shit! Shit! Shit! Eleven o'clock! How did I sleep so late? I take off my pajamas on the way to the bathroom, leaving them on the floor until the evening, when it is time to go back to bed. With the hot water supply not cooperating, I shiver through a barely warm shower, shaving only half of my legs—without shaving gel—to save time. Underarms pass the hairless test. I brush my teeth as I get out of the shower. With the toothbrush still in my mouth, I manage to apply moisturizer. After rinsing my mouth, I glance in the mirror: clean face—check; no zits—check. I finish off with mascara and a pink blush. I blow-dry my curly, thick red hair and tame it into a braid with loose curls framing my face. I race back to the bedroom where I grab my recently purchased green wrap dress that hugs me in all the right places. I finish off with nude, patent leather four-inch heels, but then decide to walk to the train station in flats and put the heels on when I get to Manhattan, knowing that otherwise, the heels will cause massive blisters. I glance into the mirror on my closet door before running out, elated with the feeling that I have accomplished a makeover in a record amount of time.

I skip down the steps, feeling giddy with anticipation. My brisk walk takes me to the station, three blocks from where I live. The station is mostly empty, since the morning rush of working crowds has already been delivered to its destination. The muffled voice of the announcer informs me that the 'M' train should be arriving in fifteen minutes; with a forty-five-minute ride to the city, I know I will be right on time. The sun reflects off of the silver shell of the train, making it shine as it pulls up closer to the platform. The car has few passengers: there is an elderly couple speaking in hushed tones, and a heavily pregnant woman with a toddler sitting on her lap, looking out the window. The mother looks completely exhausted from carrying the precious gift in her round belly. Her eyes are closed as her little one keeps saying out loud everything that he is seeing through the glass. There is a guy with a heavy backpack and headphones, completely immersed in reading a huge book, the cover of which I cannot see. I sit by the window and can't hide a slight smile as I am rocked surprisingly gently on the way to Manhattan.

The moment I step onto the platform, I am hit by the warmth of the last day of June air that is void of summer humidity. New York City greets me with the smell of food cart pretzels. My ears are assaulted with the noise of taxi honking and people chatter. The city never fails to overload my senses with smells and acoustics. I join the crowd of strangers all walking with purpose, but failing to acknowledge the purpose of each other. As I maneuver through obstacles of puddles and loitering bodies walking against the current, the human wave seems to effortlessly propel me to my destination.

CHAPTER 5

I walk into the sushi place. Its décor is modern and cold. It blends well into the concrete jungle of downtown Manhattan, adapting in order to be protected from the invisible predators that ensure the survival of only the fittest: the best restaurants. The space is dominated by the clean lines of the marble bar extending through the length of the restaurant. At the end of the bar, there is an enclosed see-through display of available fish filets. The sushi master is gliding his knife through a piece of fish, with his back slightly bent in a constant bow to his craft. The barman, dressed all in black, is busy mixing up a drink. The place is more than half full, mostly with men in dark suits who don't take their eyes off their smartphones. They eat quietly and I wonder if they even taste the food, or if it bypasses their taste buds just to fill the void in their stomachs. I look around, wondering what Max looks like. I give myself a mental smack on the forehead for failing to ask for some sort of identifying characteristic. A model-like young hostess dressed in a sleek black dress, her hair pulled back so tight I think she can't move her eyebrows, approaches me and with a soft smile, welcomes me to the restaurant.

"Good afternoon! Welcome to Orange Blossom! Are you Mila?"

"Yes," I answer, surprised.

She smiles softly again and invites me to follow her. I trail behind, trying to tiptoe so my heels don't disturb the silence of the place. She leads me across the restaurant to where the wall across the bar is covered in light grey marble; beneath its mass there is a long fireplace. The flames are seemingly floating above small crystals and fail to emanate any heat. The hostess walks fast, making a right turn at the end of the cold wall to reveal several private booths that have sliding doors made of wood and light fabric, imitating traditional partitions found in Japanese houses. She stops in front of one closed partition, slides it open, and extends her hand in a welcoming motion. I step into the booth with walls decorated in battle scenes. In front of me, there is a drawing of a town on top of a hill, protected by a wall, with a river flowing around it. The surrounding waters are crowded by fishermen's boats. The whole town is filled with people going about their structured life, protected by the walls of their symmetrical town. I can make out pairs of geishas shielded by pretty umbrellas; the town square is filled with men carrying swords and bows. The market is busy with customers shopping the rows of food.

I shift my attention from the painting, and towards the center of the room. There is a thin, black table supported by thick legs at either side, making it seem as though it is carved as one solid piece. Chairs match the table, their straight lines failing to display any signs of comfort. My gaze is interrupted by the tall figure in the left far corner. His back is to me, and he is on his cellphone, deep in conversation. He keeps his voice low, but I can make out the sharp chill of business negotiations. The hostess slides the partition behind me, leaving me to stand and stare at the back of this stranger who has somehow failed to notice my entrance.

"It has to be done today. I need the paperwork on my desk by five o'clock," he orders someone on the other side of his conversation. He is probably six feet tall, dressed in a navy suit, most likely custom-made to accommodate his wide shoulders and trim waist. The back of his head reveals the sharply cut lines of his dark brown hair.

Just as I am about to say hello, he turns around and holds up an index finger to silence my greeting. I decide to give him a minute to complete his phone call as I continue studying the intricate artwork. The wall to the left of me takes on a menacing character with its army of horsemen and soldiers marching away from a seemingly peaceful town towards some unknown battle.

"I don't care if I stab him in the back!" The dark suit continues.

I am startled by the aggressive tone of the conversation, and clear my throat to further announce my presence, but this time, my date doesn't even turn around. I stand awkwardly, clutching my pocketbook, questioning whether I should sit or stand while Max ignores me completely. I would have turned around and walked off, if it weren't for this set up by my mother. I can already hear her lecturing me on the virtue of patience, and giving people a chance. "Darling, there is no such thing as love at first sight. No one is perfect.

And if you are ready to walk off in a different direction after one bump in the road, well, there won't be an easy road to happiness." *OK Mama*, I think. *I will be patient for just a moment longer.*

He turns for a quick second and points to the wall behind me. I look over my shoulder to find a bouquet of a dozen yellow roses. Hidden within the blossoms I find a note: "Beautiful flowers for a beautiful girl." I pucker up my nose at the cheesiness of the writing, but think warmly of the gesture. Max fires off several more instructions before he finally ends the call, and shifts his attention to me.

"Hi! I am Max." He strolls towards me, hands in his pocket. He stops a few steps away, looks me up and down and then moves closer, stretching out his right hand. His handshake is weak and wet. Max does not offer an apology, but merely turns around and walks towards the table, leaving me to trail behind him.

"I hope you don't mind, but I have placed the food order so that we are not distracted," he announces without inquiring about my preferences. I cannot shake the feeling that this man is not used to rejection, or to people failing to follow his exact specifications. He sits down first, putting his phone screen-up on the table. I pull out a chair for myself, hang up my pocket book and sit down, facing my date.

"So, how are you?" he asks as he leans back and unbuttons his jacket. A rounded belly makes an appearance, no longer hidden by the well-tailored suit. I don't know what picture my mother was shown, but it was probably of a younger Max. His face, although clean shaven, is slightly puffy, revealing years of indulgence.

His lips are plump, long sausages that he licks throughout the conversation, and his teeth are blindingly white. Max's hands have a more manicured appearance than mine, and his forehead reveals no wrinkles or movement, likely from being over Botoxed.

"I am fine," I say, feeling that this blind date is a failure. I take a sip of water, looking away from Max to avoid noticing any more unattractive features. "Do you come here often?" I question, composing myself and giving him another opportunity to present a better version of himself. *Give him a chance, Mila; it's just a bump in the road. Don't run in a different direction just yet.* However, he fails to live up to any version of a decent human being when he says:

"It's kind of become my spot for blind dates. My mother fears I will end up a lifelong bachelor, so she has become my matchmaker." And *not a good one at that*, I think to myself.

"So, I guess she hasn't found the one for you yet?" I muse out loud.

"Hmm...I guess we will find out," he exclaims confidently, looking at me with a smirk. The douchebag is interrupted by two waiters who bring our food. Although I haven't eaten anything since last night, I lose my appetite on seeing what has been chosen for our consumption. A large plate of oysters and snails on ice is placed right in the center of the table.

"Mmm...," I hear Max say. "Right on time..." Without hesitating, he squeezes lemon over the oysters, grabs one, and masterfully consumes it with an unpleasant slurp. "You know that these are considered to be an aphrodisiac?"

"I think everybody knows that, but I am not a fan." I pucker up my nose.

"Try it! It might put you in the mood," he suggests, continuing to loudly slurp the oysters.

"Excuse me?!" I snicker.

"You seem a bit tense. Relax—have an oyster; have a bit of fun. Speaking of fun, I have a small gift." He lifts his napkin revealing a small, black box tied up in a pretty pink bow. Max passes it to me, but asks me to open it later, because it "ties into the theme". He says the last few words with a wink, and then licks his lips, sending unpleasant shivers down my spine. He carries on the conversation by praising himself in the most blatant ways, but avoiding looking at me directly as he aimlessly scrolls down the screen on his phone.

I quietly sip my water to keep the nausea down. I am thankful when the waiters come in with more food. I pray that there will be something I can eat to quiet my hunger. Our table is crowded with more food than we need: crab salad on top of avocado, grilled octopus, tuna sushi, salmon sushi, and variety of rolls. The waiter finishes the placement of food by topping off our glasses with Dom Pérignon, and leaving the rest of the bottle in the ice bucket by the table. Although I am surprised by the amount of aphrodisiac food, I am in utter disbelief at Max's boundless presumptuousness. I chug my Champagne before he has time to make a toast. He moves his little box with the gift inside closer to me.

"It is time to open your present. It might be something we will both enjoy." A wicked look in his eyes puts me on guard. I put down my glass and slowly open the gift. When I lift the tissue paper, I feel a bitter taste of bile in the back of my throat. The bright, pink candies are strung together in what I presume is an edible bra and panties. I jump nervously as a sudden burst of laughter emanates from Max.

"Oh, you should see your face! It is priceless! Isn't it a funny gift?! I love it!" Max throws his head back and laughs loudly, holding on to his stomach. I chug the rest of the contents of my glass; the stream of bubbles feels good going down my throat, and it gives rise to my courage.

"Is this what you always do for your blind dates? Is this some kind of buttering up feast to compensate for your unbelievable lack of tactfulness? Why don't you call it for what it is - a bad attempt at getting laid!" I yell at him as I get up.

"Sweetheart, I get laid when I want to, with whom I want to and I don't generally take them out," he sits back in the chair, sipping his Champagne. "I was entertaining the idea of settling down, getting married. So, if in the process I get laid as well, why not? You surely didn't come here expecting prince charming?"

"I am no sweetheart to you!" I throw what is left of my Champagne into his face and storm out, leaving Max sitting in his chair, frozen by my sudden attack on his mating ritual. I push back from the table, jump to my feet and grab my bag which gets caught on the back of the chair, causing it to fall.

"Baby! Where are you going?" Max questions my attempt at escape, wiping Champagne from his suit and face.

"Far away from you," I fire back, trying to free my bag from under the heavy chair.

"I like you." Max leans over and puts his elbows on his knees, watching my every move. "And when I like something, I always make it mine."

"In your dreams, asshole." I pull my bag and race towards the door. Max chases me, grabs my arm and pulls me so close that I can smell his fishy breath.

"You are feisty: exactly what I want. I will visit you soon." He smiles and looks at my mouth while licking his sausage lips.

"Let me go." I muster all my strength and pull my arm away from his tight grip. He steps back, still smirking, and rubs his chin as I reach the door which fittingly displays a large, menacing warrior beheading his enemy. The army of the peaceful city is slaughtered and the river of blood is flowing towards the town that they have left behind. This time, I run through the restaurant, stepping firmly so that the *klat klat* of my heels echoes through the place. I hold the door for a delivery man carrying a bouquet of yellow roses. I pause, recognizing the bouquet. It is the same size and wrapped similarly to the one that was gifted to me by Max. I overhear the man telling the hostess that Mr. Kogan has ordered these flowers specifically for her. She giggles, and buries her face in the flowers. Rage washes over me as I grab the bouquet from the hands of the hostess. She is so shocked by my audacity she doesn't have time to object. I find a note which reads: "Beautiful flowers for a beautiful girl."

"What an asshole!" I shove the note into the hands of the hostess and throw her bouquet on the floor.

"You tell that jerk to stick these you-know-where!" I yell as I stamp on the flowers, releasing a sweet fragrance that is all of a sudden cloyingly suffocating.

I head straight for the curb: my shivering body resonates with the anger that is seeping through my pores. The afternoon air is no longer pleasant; it hits me with a wall of humidity along with the smell of burned peanuts from the nearby food vendor, and urine from several homeless people now sleeping on the side of the building. The sidewalk is packed by an indifferent, hungry-for-lunch crowd. I plough through to get closer to the street so I can signal a cab. My confident walk is interrupted as I am rammed by something that causes my feet to buckle, sending me to the concrete. My pocketbook is thrown into the air before it spits out its insides onto the sidewalk beside me. My mind fails to give me clear directions on what I should do first: collect all my belongings, try to get up, or burst into tears from the pain of the scraped knee, or my embarrassment. One of the decisions is made for me by the stranger who caused my tumble as he pulls me up to my unsteady feet. He towers above me; in my distressed state, I can't make out the details of his appearance. All I grasp is that he is young, and athletic.

"Are you OK?" he asks, grabbing me by my shoulders, and helping me to my feet with bewilderment in his eyes. Now I collect myself enough to concentrate on his face. He has blond hair, light-colored eyes, and a trim beard. "You just threw yourself in front of me!" he shouts with both accusation and worry in his voice. He slowly releases his hands to make sure I don't tilt, and fall down again. I don't move. Still in slight shock from the situation, I watch as he proceeds to collect my belongings into my pocketbook, which he then places into my hands.

"Are you hurt?" he repeats as my eyes meet his. I just nod yes, and then no.

"Don't you look where you are going? Is this 'jerk central' here?!" I come to my senses and berate the man who stumbled innocently into the crossfire of my rage.

"Let me look at your knee; I can help." The stranger keeps his calm under my attack.

"Don't you touch me. I can help myself. Give me my bag. I have to go."

He passes me my bag and lifts his hands up slightly in surrender. I mumble how unbelievably sucky my afternoon has turned out, and throw an arm into the air to flag a taxi. A cab pulls up momentarily to take me home, saving me from further disappointments. I leave the stranger on the curb and the cab whisks me away towards Brooklyn. I sit in the confines of the cab and shake my head in disbelief at this blind date. I decide to tell my mother that I will no longer allow her to set me up with anyone, and that maybe I will refrain from any dating proposals, suggestions, or attempts forever. Unexpectedly, I start to sob uncontrollably at the sound of the weather channel predicting showers on the cab's digital screen. I can't explain what causes the tears: the release of my pent-up rage, the pain from my scraped knee, or maybe it is just the sadness that comes from confirming that romance doesn't exist anymore.

CHAPTER 6

I am safely delivered to the curbside of my house. I hand the cab driver the money, appreciating him ignoring my breakdown. I enter my pre-war apartment building, which still bears a sign on its façade identifying it as a nuclear fallout shelter, and immediately feel shielded from all the negativity of my afternoon. My legs carry me briskly up the stairs to the second floor into the safe haven of my small apartment. The humidity in my two-bedroom unit is palpable, promising a downpour that will both cleanse the streets, and renew my spirits. I share the apartment with my friend, Michelle. Our place is a mismatch of gifted and used furniture; it reflects the differences in our personalities. Based on the choices of our décor, you wouldn't imagine us as best friends. I like modern glam, and Michelle is more French country, but we have meshed our differences into the cozy comfort of true friendship.

I walk first into the tight galley kitchen and put on the kettle before proceeding into the living room to turn on the air conditioner. I collapse on the couch and stare at the ceiling, mulling over my berating of that pretentious prick, and then my disastrous spill on the streets of New York. The guy who I bounced off of must think I was either drunk, or that he ran into the clumsiest person in the city. I remember his eyes that questioned if I was hurt, and I blush now from the embarrassment. I hear the kettle whistle and my stomach grumble reminding me that I have deprived my body of any solid food since last night. Turning off the stove, I make myself a sandwich. I decide to read the next letters in my grandmother's box to distract me from my continuing misfortune in dating.

8 July, 1941

My Dearest Iskra,

Just saying your name warms up my heart. It has been two months since I have seen you. Two months since the start of the war: the longest time that we have been apart. It seems it will be an eternity before I will be able to touch you. I promise I will write. I want you to do the same. Write down everything. I want to know what you see when you wake up. I want to know what you eat for dinner. I want to know about your fears and struggles. I want to feel like I am next to you and there is no distance between us.

I have arrived to city N, a local school has been turned into the military hospital. I must say that even in a small town, bureaucracy flourishes. It took me a full day to register and get my room. The windows of my new quarters are overlooking the hospital and I am sure during peaceful days it was quite lovely to hear children going about their studies. Now the green of the summer is splattered with the grey of uniforms, cars, trucks, and people suffering.

I know you feel alone, scared and abandoned. I have an obligation, a duty to be on the front line, but I would rather be next to you. Am I being selfish? Am I a man who dreams of my own happiness before the duty to the motherland? I guess at times of war, the desire for happiness of the one man would make that man petty. I don't care. I am then petty. But I have you and the love you fill me with raises me up. I feel grand and able and courageous. And so here I am, a blabbering petty man, filled with love, ready to save the soldiers. This is how I will protect you, us. This is where I will make the most difference. I wish this war had never happened, but this is our reality and it cannot be ignored. There is nowhere to hide.

Please take care of yourself. I will see you in my dreams. I love you. Yours always, Jacob.

P.S. I hope Dar is not giving too much trouble. I know he will protect you.

12 September, 1941

My love,

I wish there was a different reality for us. I know that we all have to make sacrifices, greater sacrifices than ever. I just pray you are safe. If only the prayers could create a shield to protect you, I would pray always…harder, if that were even possible.

I wake up and fall asleep with the vision of your eyes. Your eyes of amber keep me warm; they glisten to give me hope, the light at the end of this misery.

Fall used to be my favorite season you know. I loved the rustling of the leaves under my feet as I moved through the cobblestone streets. I ran through piles and kicked them in the air. Now I am like a little rabbit shivering at the sound of any noise. I scurry through the streets begging to be unnoticed. I want to be a shadow. It is becoming easier to be a shadow. Everything is reduced to grey, cold rubble. The city is a bleak contour of what it once was.

I try to keep busy. My factory shift starts at five in the morning. I work seven days a week, twelve hours on most days. That way, the days are fleeting and go by unnoticed. This also gives me second category ration cards. Since the bombing of Badaev warehouse on September 8th everyone is afraid that rations will be reduced again. I now survive on 250 gm of green bread which appears to be mixed with saw chips.

For now, the days still provide some warmth, but I am fearful of what winter might bring. I was able to get burzhuika and store some wood. All of the wooden furniture is chopped. Only the bed, a table, and a chair remain in my room.

Dar keeps me warm at night. I am thankful for his shaggy coat. But I worry about him. People are eating anything that might have meat. Some I fear have turned to the most vile resources of staying alive. We are all starving and food is all that is occupying our minds.

My love, please be safe, you have to come back to me, safe. I love you always. Yours, Iskra.

The realization that today was a minor hiccup compared to the suffering of many people is interrupted by the sound of the door being open. My roommate, Michelle, enters—radiant from a long weekend away with her new fling.

Michelle is from Trinidad and her sunny birthplace has permanently imprinted on her bright and cheerful personality. We met during our rotations. She was finishing up her PA school, and I was on my last eight-week rotation. We bonded over our survival through schooling, laughed at crazy patient stories, had each other's back during rounds, and talked smack about the attendings-the physicians who finished all of their training and who made our life miserable. It turned out that Michelle got a job offer at the same hospital where I matched for my ER residency, and since she was already renting an apartment and her other roommate had left for a job relocation, she offered the room to me. I moved my belongings in without hesitation after calculating that I had enough money left from my loans to sustain my independent living. Of course, my parents insisted that I continue living with them, and my mother even tried shedding tears, but I insisted that I was overdue on starting my life. My mother, not having anyone else to take care of but herself and my dad, decided that she would continue taking care of me (and Michelle too) by stocking our fridge with produce and her home-cooked meals. I tried to resist, but Michelle grew so fond of some of my mother's dishes, like borsch, pelmeni, and pierogis, that she encouraged my mother to continue her feeding of us.

Michelle would often tell me, "Mila, you are book smart, but I am street smart, so pay attention and learn. If your mother wants to cook for us, then let her. It is a win-win situation for all: you don't have time to cook, and I don't know how to cook, so it saves both of us from either being always hungry or constantly eating junk. Plus, your mom is a lovely lady and I really like her." But recently, a lot of my mother's cooking has been left uneaten because Michelle has been spending less time in our cozy apartment which can only mean that she is getting serious with Rob.

Rob is a nurse from the same emergency department as Michelle, and he has been pursuing her for months. She finally relented three months ago. A few days ago, Rob took Michelle to Fire Island to meet his family and enjoy a few days at the beach.

She slowly walks into our apartment as if prolonging the return to reality. She smells of the beach and the sun. A wide smile revealing bright white teeth doesn't leave her face as she throws off her shoes and gives me the biggest hug. Michelle releases me from her embrace only to start jumping and squealing, "I love him!" She then proceeds to spin into our living room where she lands on the couch closing her eyes, and shakes her hands and feet in the air.

"Are you trying to shake off the feeling?" I tease her.

"Oh Mila! I never thought I would be a fool in love. But I am so happy!" she proclaims. "Promise me you will never use what I just said against me, or repeat it to Rob." Michelle gets serious. "He doesn't need to know that; it will go to his head." I have to pinky swear before she can smile again.

"Aww and I am so happy for you. You deserve it," I say, approving of my friend's emotions. I sit down next to Michelle, basking in her happiness. "Soooo? Details?"

"Well, the house is beautiful…right on the beach! All the siblings paid for it as a gift to their mother. She has decorated it in a nautical style. She is very nice. She told me that I was the first girl Rob had brought to meet the family. It was sooo relaxing—nothing but the beach, drinks, games, and barbeque. And my man was such a gentleman; he never left my side. I told him that I was super nervous to meet everyone and all he said was: 'Don't worry, they will love you because I love you.' Honestly, how can I not love him?" She closes her eyes. "We are going back next weekend. How about you? Did you do anything?" she asks me.

"Not much. Just had a date with a total jerk, threw Champagne in his face, ran out, tripped over some guy, fell on my ass in the city and then cried all the way back to Brooklyn." I cover my face to hide my embarrassment and giggle at the same time, thinking how ridiculous I must have looked when I fell down.

My friend's eyes widen hearing my summary of the afternoon.

"What? Girl, are you serious? I leave you for a couple of days and this is the trouble you get yourself into? Where did you find this guy? And I want to know exactly how the date went…"

"My mother set me up with him." I roll my eyes.

"Oh, I have to have a talk with your mother regarding your love life. Don't get me wrong, I love her, but she is trying to find you a husband? Honestly, I think you just need to concentrate on finding a fuck buddy."

"What?" My friend's logic doesn't make sense.

"I just don't understand how you are still a virgin! You are gorgeous and smart—how is it possible?" Michelle's voice always gets high-pitched when she raises the plausibility of my virginity.

"A redhead with glasses and braces? Not quite the attributes that were considered hot in my high school."

45

"But what about college? Everyone has sex, everyone experiments." Michelle continues to dissect my lack of sexual experience.

"I don't know." I shrug my shoulders. "I was just always studying. I told you this already."

"Yes, yes. There was a guy who wanted open relationships, right?"

"Yeah." I giggle. "I had to google what it actually meant. Another imagined that I would be a homemaker. I also had a couple of dates with this law student, but he needed to smoke weed every evening or he couldn't relax."

"Well, the last one is not so bad."

"You always say that, but you made Rob quit smoking."

"Smoking cigarettes and enjoying reefer is much different. You should try it." Michelle gives me a side eye and bursts out laughing. I throw a couch pillow at my friend and join in her laughter.

"Hmm, I think, your vagina being the virgin that she is, is sending off some weird signal. It is standing on this high pedestal and judging everyone very harshly. You know what I am saying?"

"No, I don't. You make no sense." I look at her, puzzled.

"I think because you are a virgin it puts an extra pressure on you to meet Mr. Forever, when you just need Mr. Bangmerightnow. You just need to get laid, is what I am saying. Just give me your phone; I will call your mother right now and explain that to her as well. I bet she will agree with me!"

"No, you will not! Are you crazy?" I screech.

"You know I am." Michelle stands up to search for my phone. "Where is it?" She brings me my bag. "C'mon, let me talk some sense into your mom about modern loving." She giggles and rolls her eyes at me for actually believing she would do it. "I will not call your mother. Let's Facebook the jerk you saw today."

"That is a much better idea and it requires a glass of wine, my friend." I go into the kitchen and pour us two glasses of red wine that we are always stocked with. As Michelle holds the glasses, I search the depths of my purse for my cell. Failing to find it, I turn my pocketbook upside down so all its contents are sprawled out for the second time in one day. "No, no, no!" I say in a panicky whisper. "My phone isn't here!"

"Where did you have it last?"

"I definitely had it right before I went to the restaurant, but I don't remember if I've seen it since. That guy who I bumped into—he collected all my things into my pocketbook. He probably kept my phone for himself."

"Call your cell. Let's see if he picks up." Michelle hands me her cell. I dial, and after a few rings an unfamiliar male voice picks up on the other end.

"Hi! I dropped my phone in the city today and I would like to get it back. Are you the guy who knocked me off my feet?"

"Hi! First of all, you are the one who ran into me," the pleasant and slightly raspy voice answers sarcastically. "Second of all, how is your knee?" the voice asks with a warm concern.

"Oh, it's fine, thank you. So, how can I get my phone from you? Preferably today."

"What is your name, miss? It is awkward that we are carrying on this conversation and I do not know how to refer to you."

"My name is Mila, and yours?" I roll my eyes at this annoying prolongation of conversation, but oblige to make sure I get my phone.

"Leo, it is a pleasure. I live in Brooklyn; where are you?"

"Great! Me too!" I tell Leo my address and he agrees to come by in around an hour to bring back my cell phone.

As promised, exactly one hour later, Leo rings Michelle's phone to let me know that he's downstairs. Still in my dress that I wore to the date with Max, but sticking to wearing more sensible flats and with my hair undone, I come outside to meet Leo. The streets are mostly empty— people are still hiding from the summer heat and humidity that returned after the predicted short downpour. I spot Leo as he is walking from around the corner of my building. I have a chance to look at him before he gets too close. His walk is confident, his gaze fixed on me. He is dressed in a red t-shirt and dark shorts; as he gets closer, I make out a red, foul-mouthed superhero on it. The t-shirt hugs his muscular chest and well-defined shoulders, and hangs loose around his trim waist. His hair is dark blonde and trimmed short, almost military style. He smiles widely, seemingly happy to see me. *Hmm, he's kind of cute*, I think to myself. Maybe Michelle is right: maybe I should just have fun, have sex, get it over with and enjoy life. After all, school is over, all exams are finished. I missed out on all the crazy social life of my student years…what if I regret not experiencing it—the partying, the unattached sex? I give Leo a wave when he comes closer. He looks like a great Mr. Bangmerightnow.

"Hi! How are you? That knee looks like it was taken care of." He points to the dressing on my scraped knee.

"Yeah, it's nothing; it'll heal in a couple of weeks. I'm sorry I was kind of rude to you earlier. I just really had a terrible afternoon." I blush, and put an unruly curl behind my ear.

"Don't worry—we all have those days when you just want to escape." He smiles warmly at me, accepting my apology.

"I guess. Did you bring my phone?" I decide to get to the point of our meeting.

"Oh yes! Look at me…I see a pretty girl for the second time in one day and completely lose my mind." He smiles at his own fumbling. "Here it is." He takes out my cell from his back pocket and passes it to me. I press the power button that doesn't respond. The battery is dead.

"Thanks." A pause grows between us. "Well, see you I guess!" I blurt, not knowing how to proceed. This is a bit harder than I realized; I actually have no idea how to flirt and have a guy ask me on a date.

"See you!" He turns around to walk away and I think I hear him say, "I hope."

"Hey listen—I really had a shitty day…Do you want to get a drink, or something?" I cringe at the sudden confident, unlike-me proposal. I don't have to pretend to be all cute, I decide. I am not a girl who bats her eyes, twirls her hair and drops innuendos. I will just get straight to the point and ask him out myself. What's the worst that can happen? He says no, and I don't see him again. Sure, my ego will be just a bit hurt, but there won't be any witnesses to remind me of my failure. I will get over it.

"Now?" He pauses and looks at his watch and then nods. "Let's go! Do you know any places around here?" *Wow, that was easy*, I think to myself. I didn't actually expect Leo to agree to my proposition. Well, I guess I can try and see where this little experiment will lead me.

"There is a bar a few blocks down, but I have never been there before."

"Well, let's go check it out. Lead the way." Leo steps aside so I can start us in the direction of the bar.

I feel anxious walking next to this man. I am not sure of the best pace, of the appropriate proximity, or of where to look. I choose to stare at my feet and nervously play with the curls of my hair.

"Have you lived here long?" Leo breaks the silence between us.

"No, just a few months." I shake my head, still keeping my gaze on the pavement in front of me.

"It's a nice area. I like it."

"It is. Where do you live?"

"Cobble Hill…Have you been there?"

"I've heard of it, but I've never been. The bar is right over there." I point to the building across the street as we stand at the red light to cross. Leo nods, looking in the direction I am showing him. The light turns green and Leo touches my waist lightly with his hand. I feel electricity surge through my body. The touch is brief and he puts his hand back in his pocket as soon as we finish crossing the street. We pass by a firehouse and a few small store fronts before we come to the bar. The name is "Mystic Dive." It is dark and so small that it only fits four tables along the wall opposite the long bar, and a few tables in the back. With no signs of a hostess, Leo takes the lead and heads in. I follow behind. We take seats at the bar.

"Hi!" He waves to the barman at the opposite end of the bar. "Give me a cranberry vodka please," Leo orders. "What are you having?"

"I'll have the same." I decide to stick to a simple concoction since I am not versed in alcoholic drinks. Since it is a weekday, the place is not crowded. A few older gentlemen sit at the end of the bar watching a soccer game on a TV mounted above all the bottles. Three guys still dressed in suits and ties are quietly talking about something at the table in the corner. A young bartender with a man bun quickly completes our request and offers us the menus to look at.

"I actually am very hungry; are you?"

"I am ravenous!" I admit since I haven't had a good meal for the entire day. "I could eat a cow."

We ask the man bun bartender for the specials and both decide to go with cheeseburgers.

"What were you running from today?" Leo inquires, sipping his drink.

"A really, really bad date," I admit, unashamed.

"What was so bad about it?" Leo slowly sips his drink and leans in just a bit closer. I can smell his pleasant scent of cologne.

"Oh, just about everything. From his expectations to insinuations, the guy just had a really bad vibe about him." I flinch at the memory of the terrible meeting.

"Where did you meet him? You seem like a smart, nice girl who wouldn't give an asshole any chances," he smirks.

"My mother is really overbearing sometimes and she insists on setting me up with guys constantly, so I finally relented, but never again." I take a big gulp of vodka cranberry and feel it slowly warm up my body.

"Ah, I can relate regarding overbearing mothers; totally understand." Leo nods and chuckles, taking another slow sip. "I told my mother that I do online dating so that she doesn't harass me with daughters of friends and neighbors. At least for now, she leaves me alone." He laughs and I find the sound of it very inviting. His eyes light up and small wrinkles appear in the corners showing that the smile and the laughter are completely sincere. Leo's hair, although cut short, up close reveals curls that fight to break through the rigidity of gel. The color of his eyes is hard to make out: they are brown, but so light they almost look like the color of light honey. His lips are full without being feminine, and his beard is trimmed and shaped; I imagine he looks younger without it. Leo is certainly easy on the eyes, I decide, looking him up and down as I take a last sip. I order another round since I don't feel even a little bit buzzed. I am happy when my cheeseburger arrives because I don't have to talk as much while devouring the huge monstrosity of deliciousness with a hefty side of French fries. I attack my meal right away, taming the rumbling of my stomach.

"Wow! I am impressed! You actually finished the whole thing," Leo exclaims as I lick my fingers, leaving only a few French fries on my plate. With the second drink almost finished, I feel the courage to ask Leo if he is single. Even though I have decided to look for sex and not love, I still don't want to do it with a guy who is in a relationship.

"No, I don't have a girlfriend. Are you single?" Leo inquires, still working on his cheeseburger. I am happy to hear about his lack of a significant other.

"Oh yes! And I plan to stay like that for a while!" I burst out laughing, not recognizing my own voice.

"Why is that?" Leo raises his eyebrows, as if surprised by my loud confession.

"I am just not looking for anything serious right now." I send a not so subtle hint that I am not looking for a long-term relationship. I wonder if he will take my bait and act on it. "Can I have another drink?" I ask the bartender. I can't decide whether Leo is getting more attractive as I sip more alcohol, or because the excitement of starting a fling and knowing its short-term purpose is a challenge to me.

The third drink goes down smoothly and I feel that my body is getting lighter and my movements slower. *Why haven't I had more than one drink before?* I actually feel so good, I question the years that I spent studying instead of partying like most of the students.

"How can you plan to not get serious with someone? What if you meet someone and you really like him. Will you just cut the relationship short and not get serious?" Leo questions, looking up at me from under his eyebrows while swirling his drink; his jaw tightens awaiting my answer. I decide to pursue Michelle's theory to the end and insist that I am looking for Mr. Rightnow and not Mr. Forever. Leo keeps quiet, piercing me with his eyes. Will he see through the inexperienced-in-relationships girl behind all the bravado?

"Well, I am twenty-four years old and I haven't met anyone yet." I wag my finger at Leo. "But you are pretty handsome and I like you now." I push my finger into his firm chest. The feeling of his muscles under the thin shirt sends pleasant goose bumps through my body, collecting in the pit of my belly, erupting in a thought that this would be a good time to go for a kiss. I lean towards Leo and close my eyes. I expect to meet his soft lips and lock in a passionate kiss, but when it doesn't happen, I open my eyes to find Leo's head thrown back, his Adam's apple jumping up and down, and the bar filling up with his loud laughter. The slow realization of my embarrassment detonates my anger towards Leo. He is laughing at me! I have made a complete fool of myself! I have to get out of this place. I can't even look at him anymore; all he does is laugh at me.

"I haven't met anyone like you Mila. I quite like you, but I think I better get you home." He pays for our drinks and food since I came out without my wallet, not expecting this bar trip.

"I don't need you to get me home and I don't need you to pay for my food and drinks. I will venmo you the money." I snap at him angrily, getting off the high bar stool.

"All right—you can get yourself home and you can venmo me the money. Let's go, you little fire demon." Leo gets up, puts his hands in his back pockets and rocks back and forth, waiting for me to walk first.

My drunkenness is continuing to feed my confidence, insisting that I can still function as I turn around, flipping my hair and start walking. But only a few steps away from the bar, my legs go soft and I almost hit the sidewalk again; however, Leo is there to catch me.

"Don't!" I warn him, and continue walking by myself. He nods and raises his hands in surrender, but trails just one step behind me.

We walk, or rather I try to put one foot in front of the other in somewhat of a straight line, staying silent. The walk back to the apartment is quick. I continue to mull over my failed attempt to lure Leo for a hookup, and I feel how he drills me with his eyes while probably holding back his laughter when we reach the entrance to my building.

"Let me take you up to your apartment," he says softly, putting his hand on my waist. I feel the warmth of his touch through the fabric of my dress. It sends sparks of electricity through my body, making me blush at the uncontrollable desire he makes me feel. It scares me.

"No, I told you I can get home by myself." I press my finger into the buzzer of our apartment and don't let go until Michelle picks up and lets me into the building.

"Bye!" I slam the glass door and run to the elevator to disappear out of Leo's sight as fast as I can. Thankful that the elevator opens its doors to hide me, I press my back against the corner that conceals my view of the front entrance, and take deep breaths to calm down my racing heart. The doors close and the elevator car starts the slow ride up to the second floor. *What is wrong with me? Why am I so bothered by what just happened?* I just met Leo today and I will not see him again. I wish I haven't made a complete fool of myself. I would rather the date had gone completely differently. Why did I take Michelle's advice and throw myself at him? The doors of the elevator open up and I try to push away all of these questions that I have no answer to. *This is just alcohol making your brain this crazy Mila*, I tell myself. *You will take a cold shower, have a cup of tea, and go to sleep. Tomorrow, you will laugh about this attempt at being a femme fatale.*

Michelle opens the door and she is about to say something, probably to berate me for disappearing for so long, but her face changes from concerned chastising to surprised, silent questioning of my appearance. Her mouth closes, and she lets me in.

"Don't ask. I tried following your advice and went out to get Mr. Bangmerightnow. It didn't work. I made a complete fool of myself and I think I am drunk. Don't judge me. I am going to take a shower. Please make me a cup of tea." I fire off as much information as possible in one breath, not looking directly at my friend. She doesn't say anything: no lectures, no demands for details, no accusations, no I told you so stories. Michelle, like all best friends, knows that sometimes silence is the best type of support and understanding.

She waits for me at our kitchen table with a cup of tea for her and me, and an aspirin for my headache, which I will surely have tomorrow. I wave to her as I cross from the bathroom to my room where I change into a comfortable stretched out t-shirt and sweatpants. I feel better after the cold shower; my mind is returning to clarity and logical thought. My body feels exhausted from the day's emotions and experiences. I head to the kitchen to face my friend.

"Here, take it." She passes me an aspirin and a hot cup of tea. "Do you want me to hook you up to the IV? I have everything here."

I laugh at the preparedness of my friend, shake my head no, and swallow the aspirin. I sit across from her and place my hand over the warm cup.

"I got my phone back." I try to smile and find at least something positive in my day. "And I got completely embarrassed. I think I'm just not made for dating." I put my head down on the table and my body shakes from uncontrollable laughter.

"You are so made for dating, and you are made for being loved. You are made for being appreciated, and for being made to feel special—you are made for all of that. You are smart. You have achieved so much; you are confident. There is a man who will love you for who you are, when you are ready—not when everyone else tells you it should happen. Have your tea and go to bed…you have a big day tomorrow." I nod and sip my tea. Both Michelle's words and the hot liquid make me feel warm. I repeat my best friend's words in my head, but the sound of Leo's laughter at my attempt to be kissed makes me cringe, and overshadows all the positivity that Michelle is programing into me.

"I just need to go to sleep," I say out loud and take big gulps of tea.

"I think it is a good idea."

"Good night, friend." I finish my tea and walk to the sink to wash it.

"Good night, friend," Michelle echoes. I put my cup on the drying rack and leave Michelle.

When I get to my room, I climb under the covers and decide to give my mother a call. Knowing her, she can't wait to hear all the details.

After a few rings, she picks up and as always, in her crisp almost sing-song voice she answers.

"Hello?!"

"Hi Mama."

"Oh, hello darling! Is everything all right? I have been calling you, but it goes straight to your voicemail. How was your date?" She continues to chirp, unaware of how bad my experience was.

"Really, really bad! Mama, I am going to ask you this just once: don't set me up on any more dates."

The sternness of my voice persuades my mom that I am in no mood to discuss the dating subject any longer.

"OK, honey. Of course. Are you ready for your big day tomorrow? Dad and I so very proud of you and Grandma would be as well."

"I can't wait to start, Mama."

"Let me know when we can come visit. I will bring some food for you and Michelle, and we will celebrate."

"I will. Love you."

"I love you too. Have a good night, darling!" She hangs up the phone and I know she perceives this conversation only as a temporary failure in her quest to see me successfully dating.

I go to bed hoping for a restful night, but instead, I am overcome with anxiety thinking about the start of my residency. I toss and turn, anticipating the arrival of my first day when I can start making a difference. The long years of studying fade against a seemingly endless night. I collapse into sleep and my last vision is of the man who stole my phone and then laughed at my attempt to kiss him.

CHAPTER 7

The realization that I wanted to be become a physician came to me when I was in high school. My grandfather was diagnosed with cancer of the stomach; he had his stomach removed, as well as part of his esophagus. He could no longer eat normal meals, only purees in small amounts, and he didn't enjoy it. The cancer spread. He had constant regurgitation; his colon was rerouted to the outside of his belly. A colostomy bag became part of his bodily functions. Doctors suggested chemotherapy. I saw how this once active, talkative man slowly withered away and turned into a gaunt, motionless figure waiting in bed to draw his last breath. He didn't want any more treatments. He didn't respond to my grandmother and my mother begging him to go see a doctor.

I remember him saying to me, "Mila, I have lived my life. I don't want poking and probing—and for what? So, I can get a couple of months to just exist and suffer? Talk to your grandmother for me, darling... I know she is suffering, but I cannot battle this any longer and I cannot witness her futile efforts to change my mind."

I couldn't understand how disease can just change a person...how it can take away the desire to live. I decided then that I would go to medical school to better understand life and death, and perhaps gain the ability to enable a person to fight for his or her life.

My grandfather died quietly. The evening before his death, he seemed to be in better spirits. He got up and walked to the bathroom, which he hadn't done in weeks. My grandparents slept in different bedrooms and my grandmother says she didn't hear him calling her; she didn't hear moaning, or any sounds of distress. In the morning, she found my grandfather dead. She still wishes that he had called for her for a final goodbye. I cried: it was the first death I had experienced. The realization that this person, who was part of all my life, was no longer with me made me better understand the brief moment of our existence, and how much or how little of an impact we could make. So, I studied. There was no-one more studious than me. I finished school with a 4.0 average at sixteen years of age. I excelled in pre-med and much to the satisfaction of my parents, stayed in New York to attend NYU medical school. I decided to become an emergency room physician. I wanted the action, and I wanted the fast pace. I wanted to make a difference, swiftly, for as many as possible, in the best way possible.

CHAPTER 8

I jump from the invisible nudge. It is still dark outside, but my sleep flees into the night, leaving me surprisingly energized. I lie in bed collecting my thoughts from the previous day and get embarrassed all over for my drunken behavior with Leo. I wonder if I had been myself—if I hadn't tested Michelle's theory—would he be interested in getting to know me? I felt an attraction to him that I don't remember ever feeling before. But all I probably did was to make him run for the hills. I sigh and slowly climb out of bed with my head still feeling heavy from yesterday's cranberry vodkas.

I shuffle into the kitchen where the clock on the microwave shows 4:30 a.m. I raise my eyebrows in surprise and thank my internal clock for giving me a head start. I put on the coffee pot and prepare myself instant oatmeal. My anticipation of the upcoming day builds with every drop of coffee that I hear. All of a sudden, my skin erupts with small electrical impulses and my ears start to burn. Even my body knows how important today is. I have my breakfast in what seems to be deafening silence. Even the streets are still asleep, tired from servicing drivers and pedestrians. In just a little bit, Brooklyn will slowly wake up. The silence will be abolished by the noise of sirens and the honking of aggressive drivers. I decide to pick up the letters to pass the time.

17 October, 1941

Jacob, my love,

I feel that it is pointless to ask a mundane "How are you?" I know of the horrors you face. I feel guilty adding the burden of my wretched existence, but we promised to share good or bad to stay connected, so here it goes.

Life here cannot be even called an existence; it is survival on the most primal level. I am up before the sun and fall asleep when it has already hidden behind the horizon. I am afraid if I stop moving that I will freeze to death. Thank God for Dar who is my means to survival in this vicious, early, cold winter. It seems that the weather wants to envelope everything into eternal cold, hoping that it can stop the brutality of the war and hide the ugliness of the destruction in a pure white blanket. But it only becomes another enemy. The streets are reduced to rubble, though our building is left undamaged. Most windows are still intact. The survivors set up a bomb shelter in the basement of our house. I have a bed, a few books, and an oil lamp that keeps me occupied during the days and nights of bombardments. It is strange how people just go about their life as the Germans are pounding Leningrad. September was the most devastating for the city—the bombings didn't seem to stop. People were affected at first by the sheer level of noise. We separated temporary living quarters with some curtains and blankets to preserve what is left of our privacy.

Yesterday, I found an oak leaf; it was completely red. I remembered my last birthday before the war. You brought twenty white roses and one that was red. "This red rose is for my true love, the only one who makes my heart burn, my spark in the cold world," you whispered in my ear. This memory made the day seem less dark and bleak.

I leave Dar at home when I go to the factory. He is getting too weak to go up and down even a couple of flights of stairs. He has lost weight. At the factory, I am a machine. Sometimes I imagine that the factory is one big mechanical being and we are little components, wheels and pistons, emotionless, working until we break down beyond repair. And most of us do break down. There are hardly any men left. They perish…preferred prey of the ever-hungry war.

I think I can do my work with my eyes closed. I am hoping that the weapons I build help to protect you, and speed up the victory against Germany. I hope—that is what keeps me going. I hope to see you; I hope to look into your amber eyes and find the same love and tenderness there; I hope we can be. Please, stay safe. Do not despair. I love you. There is nothing that will stop me from fighting to stay alive. Yours always, Iskra.

~

23 October, 1941

My beautiful, strong Iskra,

I didn't know that my yearning for you could be any stronger, that my love for you could still grow. But with each passing day, I realize that you are my salvation. I see death all around me: people in pain, begging for help, and I am all but helpless in their suffering. The thoughts of you keep me sane. The memories of us remind me of a different life—a life that is so recent, and I cannot but hope that it is still possible to go back to it.

Our troops are moving deeper into the motherland. The orders are to not give up a centimeter of land. The men, or rather boys, who haven't had a chance to become men, lie in piles, failing to withstand the Nazi's well-organized, ruthless offensive.

Sometimes we have a few days of quiet where we can better take care of the wounded and avoid turning into butchers. But butchers we are when there is active fighting. We triage patients in seconds, deciding who is already beyond saving, and who still has some fight in them. Amputations are a common occurrence. Sometimes we succumb to brutality and just chop, chop, and chop away: legs, hands, arms.

How naive I was in the beginning—as a surgeon, I was looking forward to the battle. I was like young Petya from War and Peace who couldn't wait to kill his first enemy, only to be killed before he could feel his purpose as a soldier fulfilled. My pride of being a surgeon is tarnished by this war. I am so tired of death, of human flesh. I don't even know if I am helping anyone. I disassemble, saw, and chop. I don't see people anymore; I don't hear their screams. I just put parts together and make sure they function, but I don't see the person who I am treating.

I wonder if you will be disappointed by the man I have become. I know I don't recognize the man in the mirror anymore. What I would give, to go back to our life before the war.

I imagine when we meet again…It will be summer; it will be quiet. We will have no words to say, because pain and suffering do not need a voice. I will hug you tight and breathe in the smell of your hair. We will stay like this for a long time, and then we will make plans for our future, and never speak about this darkness.

I love you Iskra, please do not forget that. Yours, Jacob.

I stop reading the letters. The suffering is hard to imagine. The outlook is bleak. These two people were changed by the war—their world collapsed, but their love persevered. The clock shows 5:00 a.m., and I know I have to start getting ready.

After breakfast I take a shower, which fails to put out the tingling of my skin. I put my hair into a ponytail and apply mascara and a little bit of blush. I keep my outfit simple with black pants and a striped blue shirt that has a thin tie-belt around the waist. Michelle finds me nervously flipping through channels in our living room at 5:30 a.m.

"What time did you get up?" she murmurs in her half-asleep state.

"Four-thirty. I couldn't sleep any longer. There is coffee and if you want, I can make you oatmeal while you are getting ready." I make the offer in order to keep myself and my nerves busy.

"Sure, doc—I won't say no to that. I'll be in the shower." Michelle walks off and I busy myself preparing her breakfast. I wait for my friend so we can drive in together. She gets ready, humming a familiar song, but I can't remember the words for it. I try to block it with the news of the day on the TV, but the tune gets stuck in my head. Michelle wears green scrubs that the staff gets from the dispensing machine at the hospital, and sparkly blue Crocs that she says make her feel like Cinderella, walking on clouds.

"Let's go, doc…Patients are waiting; lives need to be saved," she says teasingly, and we head out at 6:00 a.m.

I finally make out the words that my friend is singing. It's a seventies' song about "stayin' alive" and it keeps running on repeat in my head until we reach the hospital.

Except for the low humming along to the songs playing on the radio, Michelle is keeping quiet. Is she sensing my anxiety before my first day, or is she re-playing her lovely getaway in her head? I don't want to ask and break a rare silence between us.

We park in the parking garage and make our way to the hospital via a tubular, plexiglass walkway. The walkway is connected to a small room with an elevator that takes us to the emergency department located on the first floor of the hospital.

As soon as the doors of the elevator open, I imme-diately recognize the familiar smell of bodily fluids and medications competing with an underlying smell of sterility. Strangely, I never feel any aversion to it. The smell gets stronger when we open the double doors into the emergency department, and now it is strengthened by the orchestra of medical staff speaking in hushed tones, as well as the loud moaning and screaming of some patients, and the rhythmic beeping of various technology that some of those patients are connected too.

"Nervous?" Michelle asks as I take in the view before me.

"Not anymore. I finally made it here," I tell her as I feel my breath steady, my heart slow, and the anxious ringing in my ears disappear.

"That's my girl!" Michelle gives me an approving squeeze of my arm. "Now, I have to check if I have any students with me today. You should go change into your scrubs. You know where to get them, right?" I nod, remembering the long hallway that leads to the changing rooms with the scrub dispensing machine. "The attendings usually start the rounds by the nurses station and if you need me, I am on the other side. Good luck and stay out of trouble." My friend pats my shoulder as she bestows her last pieces of advice, and walks away.

I find Dr. Kim by a computer. He looks disheveled and puffy, but able to concentrate on typing a note on one of the patients. Dr. Kim is thin and tall. He wears large glasses that look heavy; they slide down his nose and he frequently puts them back with his finger only for them to slide down again a few short moments later.

"Good morning, Dr. Kim," I greet him. "How are you?" He turns his head to me and for a moment, looks puzzled by my persona. His blank stare quickly turns into recognition.

"Dr. Roth—welcome, welcome. I am just finishing up my notes so we can start the rounds. Your first day, huh? Best of luck. I think your second-year resident should be here shortly. Dr. Patel and Dr. Renner will take over for me." He returns to typing the note and I go to the resident's lounge to drop off my pocketbook and pick up my green scrubs. As I walk to the room, I search through my bag for a pen, but it always seems to swallow any objects that I require. My search keeps me so occupied that I inadvertently walk into someone, but this time I am able to firmly keep my feet on the ground. I look up to begin my apologies for my clumsiness and find myself staring into familiar, warm, honey-colored eyes.

Shit! How is it possible?! My embarrassment washes over me in a cold wave of sweat. He is wearing green scrubs…he must be working here. This is the worst thing that could have happened. I should stick to studying, and not testing dating theories! Thank God, at least I didn't sleep with him, only made a complete, childish, drunken fool of myself, and now actually have to face him again.

"Mila! Hi! What are you doing here?" he lights up in a smile. "You have a knack for running into people. What is wrong with you? You should have a blinking warning sign: 'possible sudden obstacle, watch out!'" Leo jokes. He is always joking, laughing, and smiling. Why am I so bothered by it?

"Hi! What are you doing here? This is so bizarre. I didn't expect to see you…again." I bite my lip. I am actually happy to see him, but feel completely embarrassed about my behavior last night. My happiness changes into concern over the realization that we are working in the same building. I cannot possibly get romantically involved with anyone here. "Listen, please forget what happened yesterday. I wasn't myself.

I never behave like that or drink like that, ever. I just don't want any awkwardness between us." I suggest to him. Why does he have to work here? If I ran into him anywhere else, I would love to be more than just cordial; but for now, I need to run away, escape and just act professional. Hopefully, I don't see him much.

"You run into me again and again and you don't apologize?" he says with a slight smirk.

"I am sorry. I have to run. Please just forget what happened, OK?" I plead with him.

"Let me take you out on a proper date and all will be forgiven." He looks at me with his sunny gaze and I get cautiously excited.

"You want to go out with me, even after I behaved the way I did?" I start to question his intentions. What is he looking for? Does he remember that I told him I am not looking for anything serious, and is that the reason he wants to go out? I should explain to him that I was just testing a theory.

"I told you I liked you…I was being honest. I would like to get to know you. How about I make it completely stress free? Since I will be stuck in the hospital for the next twelve hours, let's meet in the cafeteria for lunch and just chat. Then you can make a decision about going on a real date." His offer sounds innocent enough. I wanted to make a better impression on him; here is my chance. This is not even a real date. We are just having lunch at work.

"And if it doesn't work out? What then? We will be miserable coming to work and having to face each other." I try to stand my ground on principal, but the ground is getting shaky under the influence of his gaze.

"Don't worry, I can handle rejection," Leo says in his usual confident tone.

Can I take a chance on his offer? He saw me at my worst, and is still interested in me. "It is not a date— this is just a lunch, and if I don't want to go on a real date you need to promise me there will be no sad stares in my direction, or any uncomfortable behavior from you—OK?" I lay out my conditions, pointing my finger at him.

"Agreed!" he extends his arm for a shake to seal the deal.

"Great then!" this time I get a chance to smirk and shake his hand firmly. "Here is my phone number. Text me when you are going down to have lunch and I will try to join you." I scribble my phone number and hand it to him. "OK, see you later!" I give him a little wave and hurry off to get my scrubs. I run into the changing room and feel my heart beating fast. This unexpected meeting with Leo makes me giddy with excitement. I decide to try and tuck away that excitement for now since I don't want it to interfere with my first day of obligations and duties. I get my scrubs from the dispensing machine. They come out in a tight roll which I unravel and stare at: this is the uniform that I have earned with years of studying. I put it on and run my hands over the fabric. Dr. Roth, you finally made it! I put my white coat over the scrubs and clip my hospital badge over my pocket. My work outfit is adorned with a stethoscope over my neck. Now I am ready to see the patients.

When I return to the ER, I find Dr. Kim, Leo, and Dr. Patel standing together engaged in cheerful conversation.

"Dr. Roth—let me introduce you: this is Dr. Renner. He will be your attending, and he is great at teaching residents the tricks of the trade." Dr. Kim points to Leo. "Dr. Renner this is Dr. Roth. She is a first-year resident, starting her first day." He makes my introduction so official that I feel myself blush.

Oh shit! This has gotten so, so much worse that I could have imagined. I extend my hand to Leo for another shake. I don't want to explain to the others our previous run-ins, and decide to make it as nonchalant as possible.

"We already met, but it is a pleasure." I manage to say and feel stupid that I didn't ask Leo what his job was in the hospital. *What do I call him now? Leo? Doctor?* I question myself.

"Pleasure is mine," he replies with a sly smile that makes my body warm. I feel my cheeks burning.

"Excellent!" Dr. Kim continues, not noticing my reticence. "And you already know Dr. Patel from your orientation."

I give a nod to Doctor Patel. Dr. Patel takes his second-year position very seriously. He disapproves of jokes on the job, he disapproves of actions that take precedence over the job, and he disapproves of anyone who thinks of anything other than the job. I hope he hasn't noticed me blush at the introduction to Leo, for he would certainly disapprove of that as well.

"Let's begin," Dr. Kim suggests and we all follow his command and look at our flow sheet. Dr. Kim goes over the list of the patients, most of who are either waiting to be discharged or waiting to be admitted. Several patients are still waiting for their test results. Those results would determine whether they stay in the hospital, or are released.

I concentrate on making notes next to the patients' names on my list, but feel the gaze of Leo drilling into me, inconspicuous and unapologetic. I bring my head down lower and press the pen harder to the paper. Why did I have to run in to him and agree to meet him for lunch? And why is he looking at me like that? He's probably thinking that I am some naïve, first-year resident that he can take advantage of…I hope he will not make my life miserable.

CHAPTER 9

The emergency department of my hospital is the busiest in the city. It is also a level one trauma unit, and there is rarely a week without either a gunshot wound or stabbing. ED is divided into several sections: pediatrics, trauma, obstetrics and gynecology (or OBGYN), and fast track. All services are covered by residents. Fast track, where simple emergencies are taken care of, and OBGYN are also serviced by Physician Assistants. Each shift lasts twelve hours and during that shift, a particular section of ED has an attending, plus a first, and second year resident. Third year residents rotate between day and night shifts. Night shifts for first year MDs start one month into the residency, to give enough time for the newbies to get some experience and become more independent. Nobody babysits a first-year resident—one is thrown into the ocean of medicine and either adapts, or struggles to stay afloat. The procedures are done quickly: you see one, you do one, and then you teach one—a mantra memorized and passed down by the generations. Rounds occur at 7:00 a.m. sharp every day. Residents crowd near the attending physician, who spits out details of the patient's history and complaints, and then the residents are drilled with questions. Some attendings choose to torture and humiliate the residents; some pass on the knowledge eagerly, feeling sympathetic to the struggles of the newly minted physicians. Today, I am slated to stay in the general part of ED. We will split patients with Doctor Patel, who will see the more complicated ones. I will see to the straightforward complaints, and then present them first to Doctor Patel, and then to Dr. Renner.

Ms. Mary Joe, or "MJ" as she prefers to be called, is a petite Filipino nurse with at least twenty years of experience in both treating patients, and bossing staff around. She presents the first patient to me.

"Dr. Roth—congrats on your first day," she says without much enthusiasm. "Here is your first victim." A chuckle escapes her lips. "Fifty-five year-old pink puffer in room five: denies current smoking…says she quit five years ago; two pack a day, twenty-year history. She presents with shortness of breath."

I take my first case and feel surprisingly calm. I reread her intake form, review her vitals, and form a differential diagnosis without yet seeing her. My thoughts are crisp, and my brain reviews the information methodically. My grey matter doesn't hesitate…It suddenly gets to practice the knowledge that I have stored during all the years of studying. When I go in to see this patient, I am met by a huffing and puffing thin woman, whose skin is pink from being starved of oxygen. She sounds like a balloon about to burst if she doesn't release the extra air.

"Hello, Ms. Leola. My name is Dr. Roth. I will be seeing you today."

"I don't need you to see me: I need you to make me better." She puffs out, frustrated; her chest labors hard, but little air is inhaled. She has to lean forward, supporting her upper body with arms pressed tightly against her knees - the classic tripod position of an emphysema patient.

"Well, let me examine you first so we can treat you appropriately." My offer leaves her dissatisfied, but she only sounds like a balloon that cannot take flight and escape this ED. She surrenders to my exam. I start by looking at her face: it is covered in a net of dilated capillaries; even her sclera seems to have developed extra blood vessels, hoping to deliver more oxygen to starved tissue. She pushes out the air slowly through her pursed lips. Her eyes, nose, and mouth exams are all unremarkable. My fingers don't palpate any enlarged lymph nodes. I ask for her permission to listen to her lungs and examine the rest of her body. She gives me an approving puff before I proceed to listen to her carotids to screen for bruits, the presence of which will indicate that she is at risk of a stroke. I hear a rhythmic, unobstructed whooshing of blood in her left carotid, and I quickly decide that it is completely normal; the auscultation of the right one makes me pause and listen a little longer. I think I hear something, but I can't tell with certainty if it is a true bruit. I make a mental note of this finding so I can write up the order for the ultrasound. I then listen to her lungs, imagining what they look like: instead of soft, spongy, uniform texture, her lungs are dilated into multiple blebs, distended and threatening to burst. I feel sorry for the strain that this woman's body is under.

"Let me discuss your condition with Dr. Renner, and we will come back and let you know what our next step is, OK?"

"Pffft." The aggravated sound escapes her mouth accompanied by a roll of her eyes.

I go to the nurses station, input my orders for Ms. Leola, and take the next patient. Ever-present Ms. MJ reports: "Obese female; forty years old, in room seven. Complains of drilling back pain and nausea; urine pregnancy is negative." Her brief description gives me a clue to the possible diagnosis of my patient. The four F's: female, forty, fat, and fertile usually predispose a patient to gallstones, which are accompanied by symptoms of nausea and pain that radiates to the back. I go to the room with a mental list of questions that I have formed based on Ms. MJ's presentation.

"Ms. Holestein? Hi! My name is Dr. Roth, I will be taking care of you." I introduce myself to a woman who appears to be grimacing from pain, but manages to smile.

"Hi. How are you? Can you tell me what is wrong with me? Is it cancer?" The last question is pronounced in a whisper.

"Let me take a look at you first, and we will run some tests before we jump to conclusions." I try to avoid feeding her paranoia with any doubt, or a direct answer prior to having all information before me.

"Oh Lord, please let it not be cancer!" She sends her request to the higher power. I start my exam from the head and as I go down, poking and probing parts of her body, I question my patient on when the pain started, whether anything has made it better or worse, and if the pain travels, or stays in one area. She manages to answer all of my questions, giving me a stronger suspicion that this is indeed a case of gallstones. I inform her of my possible diagnosis, but warn her that more tests are needed to confirm this. Relief at not hearing a mention of cancer in the differential relaxes the frown on her face.

"I knew our Lord would help!" she proclaims, gesturing a cross over her chest. She grabs my hand and whispers, "Are you a believer, Dr. Roth?"

"I am not religious," I answer her.

"I will pray for you." Ms. Holestein informs me. "The love of our Lord will shine upon you!" she raises her eyes to the ceiling, closes them, and starts to mumble a prayer.

"Thank you!" I say to her softly and leave her be to talk to the one above.

I want to present the cases to Doctor Patel and Leo, but can't find the second-year resident anywhere, so I go to Leo directly. He is standing by the nurses station, charting his notes.

I clear my throat to announce my presence.

"Dr. Renner? I have a few patients to discuss with you." It is strange seeing him in the white coat over scrubs, and not being able to call him by name. He looks taller; there is also a boundary that is created by the uniform, and the new name. He turns his whole body towards me and I notice a smirk in his eyes. I imagine he's waiting for me to mess up so he can make fun of me.

"Mila—it is certainly amusing to run into you in the most unexpected of places. I am actually looking even more forward to our lunch now."

"I have to cancel…I certainly didn't anticipate that we would be working together like this." I try to say it without revealing any disappointment and regret. I want to say that I wish we had met under different circumstances, but I decide that it is best not to give any impression that I was interested in him. "I want to assure you that I will keep our relationship strictly professional, and I would hope that I can expect the same from you. You can refer to me as Dr. Roth, and I will refer to you as Dr. Renner. I think it will help to avoid the familiarity between us." Looking straight into Leo's eyes, I deliver the speech that I have been mulling over in my mind ever since I found out that he was my attending.

My words erase his smile. The disappointment is evident, but he quickly hides it behind furrowed brows; his eyes darken. The silence lasts for what seems like minutes.

"Sure, Dr. Roth—I can do what you are asking. I understand your concerns if we were to go out. I am an attending and you are my resident. I told you: I am not a sore loser." He tries to smile, but turns away and continues to type on the keyboard. "Now, you can tell me about your patient," Leo says in a cold, emotionless tone, devoid of the warmth I was getting used to hearing. I hope he is being honest about not being a sore loser…I wouldn't want him to be the vengeful type of physician who punishes me for refusing to go out with him. I fire off my cases with a slight tremble in my voice and wait for his judgment on my diagnoses, and proposed treatments.

"Dr. Roth, do you think Ms. Leola is an active smoker?"

"No, she denied that," I reassure him. "She told me she quit five years ago."

"Dr. Roth—I will let you in on a little secret, so that you can save yourself some grief and disappointment. Do not trust your patients—ever. They will want to please you. They all lie…some intentionally, some not. To prove this, I can bet you a cup of coffee that your patient is huffing because she is puffing." I look at Leo, surprised, not believing how cynical his outlook is, but do not argue his theory. We go together to see the pink puffer, but when we enter the room the bed is empty, and all but the presence of her pocketbook reminds us that she was here.

"It seems to me that you have lost your patient, Dr. Roth; call me when you manage to find her." Leo looks at me—I think he smiles with the corners of his mouth. He is definitely laughing at me. He walks off, leaving me feeling embarrassed about the missing patient on my first day of residency. I ask nurses passing by and PTAs if they have seen her, but only all-knowing Ms. MJ sends me outside to the ambulance dock.

The dock is the known spot for smokers, but I don't give up hope that my patient is just taking a walk, or talking on the phone. My hopes disappear like smoke into thin air when I get to the dock. Ms. Leola is sitting on the bench, enjoying a cigarette.

I go back into the ER to let Leo know that he was right, but instead, I question out loud: "Why would she do it? How can she do it to her body?" I don't know if I am looking for an explanation from Leo, or trying to find the understanding within myself.

"You're trying to rationalize the irrational," Leo says. "Patients often look for an instant relief so they can go back to what they were doing before the discomfort, the hurt, and the pain. To them, it doesn't matter that it caused them to be here. They receive their only pleasure from these destructive processes and they are willing to pay, whatever the cost. Wouldn't you give anything just to feel happy?"

"I don't think destruction can bring happiness or pleasure. I think the destruction is how people escape. Destruction is easy…Creation: that is work; hard work. Some people are just too scared to try something different, something unfamiliar. It's hard to confront failures, but we have to continue to believe that one day, they will succeed. Believing in someone is a form of healing and I am here to heal." Leo cocks his head slightly to the side and his warm eyes peer so deeply inside of me that I have goose bumps from the reach of his gaze.

"Get Ms. Leola back to her bed," he orders with a sudden iciness in his voice as he walks off into the depths of the ER.

I return to the dock. When Ms. Leola sees me, she rolls her eyes and puts out the half-smoked cigarette.

"Why did you do it?" I ask her, trying to ignore Leo's theory. "We are trying to help you, and you just stomped all over our efforts."

"I don't need anyone's help," my defiant patient says, looking into the distance.

81

"Oh yes, but you do, or you wouldn't be here. You can barely breathe; I don't even know how you were able to walk this far. And all this for a cigarette? Does it mean so much to you that you're willing to lose your life? Is it easier to keep living from cigarette to cigarette than to accept help?" My questioning is met by silence and lack of eye contact. "Sometimes you have to accept the helping hand. We are here for you, but we can't get you better if you don't cooperate."

"What are you, new or something?" she tries to maintain a tough, don't bother me attitude as she looks directly at me for the first time.

"Let's get you in the room so we can continue with your treatment," I press. She rolls her eyes again, but this time, it is a roll of defeat and I now know that she will be willing to accept help. I bring out a wheelchair to transfer her back to the room. I finish connecting her to the pulse oximeter as Dr. Renner comes into the room and, not lifting his eyes off the chart, he poses a question to the patient that makes me freeze at the coldness of it.

"Ms. Leola—when do you want to die?" I see my patient shutting down the door of trust that I was able to barely crack open as she hears the question. "Because this is how it is going to happen: I will send you for a CT scan, then we will have a surgeon come see you, but I don't need to see the results to tell you that you have destroyed your lungs. They are filled with useless air sacs that can't wait to rupture. I will start you on the steroid drip for now, until surgery is able to see you, and then you will be transferred to their service. It also seems that your carotid artery developed a bruit, which means it is cutting off circulation to your brain and you are at risk for developing a clot. If that clot dislodges, you will suffer a stroke." He doesn't let the patient utter a word before he turns around, leaves the room, and shuts the door to the room and to the patient.

"You see? All I get is the verdict...A punishment." She sinks her head into the pillow; she no longer looks at me. Her eyes are transfixed on an invisible spot on the ceiling.

"This is your reality. Dr. Renner just wants you to understand the seriousness of your condition. He is not here to punish you. But if you don't care, nobody will. First, you have to love yourself, so you are able to do better for your health." I say what first comes to my mind, hoping that she will take my words seriously and consider changing her attitude. I leave the patient and find Leo typing orders for Ms. Leola. His fingers press the keys vehemently, as if he tries to force the words onto the computer against their will. For the first time, I notice etched-in lines across his forehead and between his eyebrows. His thick, blond eyelashes frame tired looking eyes. His lips are full with a beautiful cupid's bow that begs to be stroked. His sharp jaw is supported by a chin with a slight dimple in the middle of it— visible even through the short stubble of the beard. His wide shoulders are rounded by the years of invisible burden. He takes off his white coat and I see the defined muscles and ligaments of his hands and forearms. He looks so strong, but for some reason, I sense such vulnerability that I have to fight off the desire to give him a hug. I bravely march up to question his approach with Ms. Leola.

"That was a little harsh...I think she needed a little more love than toughness." Leo looks up at me and I hold back saying any more, for he looks so severe.

"Dr. Roth, when you are an attending you can approach your patients any which way you want. I believe some patients deserve a kick in the ass to wake them up, and see that they are on the brink of death. That patient is a regular in this ED. I have witnessed her failure to give up smoking too many times." He turns back to typing, and I keep looking at him, trying to decide if I should say anything else.

"Oh, I didn't know you had treated her before," I confess. He just lets out a long sigh of exasperation. Our tense silence—him establishing his superiority and me admitting my novice mistake—is broken by Dr. Patel. He rushes towards us and stutters for a second.

"Doc, Dr. Renner...I need your help. My patient is not cooperating and I can't get any history from him."

"What do you have so far, Dr. Patel?"

"He was brought in by the ambulance with the complaint of shortness of breath and constipation. He refuses to lay down; diaphoretic. He demands to see the main guy before he reveals any more information and he doesn't let me perform the exam. He scared off all the nurses."

"Well, let's go see this patient of yours, then. Dr. Roth, I placed the order for the ultrasound of Ms. Leola's carotids. Please contact surgery for consult and make sure she gets IV Prednisone. Join us afterward. Let's see if we can elicit any more information from Dr. Patel's patient."

I do what I am told and then find Dr. Patel and Leo by the uncooperative patient's room. When we enter, we are met by a muscular, tanned patient lying on his side. He is covered in colorful tattoos on both of his arms and extending up to his neck. His hair is dark and cut with precision with a lightning bolt design on the left side of his scalp. He has a large claw-like piercing in his left ear. The hospital gown looks too small for his broad shoulders and thick neck, and he is holding the bottom of the gown as he lies on his side so it doesn't slide down. In his chart, he is listed as Joseph McMann, 38 years of age. Small beads of sweat are frozen on his forehead; he is motionless.

"Are you the main guy?" he asks, wincing in pain and slowly breathing out through pursed lips.

"I am Dr. Renner. Can you please let us examine you so we can figure out how to help you?" Leo gets straight to the point. The patient shakes his head.

"Man, you don't need to examine me. I will tell you what happened, but get that Indian dude out of here; he makes me uncomfortable," he manages to say in one breath.

"Listen to me, Mr. McMann. This is a teaching institution. These residents are here to learn and to help you, so everyone stays," Leo says firmly.

"I have a dildo in my ass. All right! All right!!!" he tries to scream out and then grunts, grabbing his stomach. "I tried to get it out, but it is too much fucking pain and I felt like I would pass out."

"Where is your partner?" Leo questions.

"I was alone, dude."

"It is Dr. Renner," Leo corrects his familiarity.

"Whatever, doc. I like to enjoy alone time. I am not gay: I have a wife. But she came home too early and she's never seen me doing this, so I freaked out. I had nowhere to hide it." As the patient presents his story, Leo is able to listen to his chest and heart and gently palpate his abdomen without much objection from the patient.

"How long is it?"

"It is long. It is double-sided," he says with a tremble in his voice, but managing to hold back the tears.

"Get bedside X-ray, stat. Call surgical consult now. I want them to meet me here." The urgency in Leo's voice or the pain from the dildo make Mr. McMann cry. He has to restrain the sobs—his tears, and the clear mucous from his nose run freely down his face.

"Is it serious, doc?"

"I don't know how serious yet, but I am concerned about possible organ damage and we have to see how to take it out. Are you OK lying on your side? Dr. Patel, please put in the orders." Dr. Patel nods and hurries out of the room. Leo addresses the patient again. "Is your wife here, by the way? Do you want me tell her anything?" The patient shakes his head no.

"I told her that I just have a bad case of constipation. I don't want her to know anything. I sent her home," Mr. McMann manages to inform us.

"OK, let's wait for the X-ray and a surgical consult and then we'll have a clearer plan on how to proceed." The patient grunts in agreement and lays his head down on the bed, wiping off the tears. Leo motions for me to step out and when we do, he asks me to call for a surgical consult while he goes to check on other patients. We meet back by the patient's room a few minutes later and I see the tech already wheeling the portable X-ray out of the room, where Mr. McMann continues to grunt and moan.

"Come—the film is already in the system. I will pull it up on the screen so we can look at it together with the surgeon." We walk to the nurses station and find an unoccupied computer. While pulling the patient's chart on the screen, Leo continues. "Get used to finding objects in the anal cavity. I think there is a stack of X-rays somewhere around...You can look through them, I promise you will be amazed by some people's will, and stretch," Leo says with a corner smile, a sign that the ice-cold disposition he has been displaying since I told him about our strictly professional relationship is thawing a bit. As Leo bestows upon me the wisdom of an ER attending, I cannot shake off the feeling of failing to see him as an attending...As my superior. It is OK to like him, right? right??? My heart stirs at this thought. But my brain quickly silences the feeling of self-approval with a vision of how inappropriate it would be. *What is wrong me? Mila, get a hold of yourself! Don't become the pathetic story of a resident falling for her attending. Sure, he's handsome, but you have just been alone for too long, and your body is playing tricks on you. You are a resident—there is no time for it, and these thoughts are completely improper.*

My battling heart and brain are forced to put down arms when I spot the box labeled: "anal objects". I open it, pull out X-ray images, and hold them up to the light; to my surprise, I find that patients were able to insert jars, Christmas lights, and workout weights inside their anal cavities. I put the images down when I spot a surgical team walking towards us. I am introduced to Dr. Grim, the surgeon, and two of his surgical residents who acknowledge my presence with a nod, but shake hands only with Leo. They are all dressed in green scrubs tucked into their pants; they don't wear stethoscopes. I am sure they each have a scalpel in their pocket, just in case something needs to be cut. Unlike his last name, Dr. Grim doesn't have anything grim about his appearance…He looks more like Santa Claus with a white beard and combed back white hair. I wait for him to erupt in "ho-ho-ho". His humor befits a bad Santa as it is peppered with racy jokes.

"What do you have for us? I heard it is a bad ass case." He chuckles at his own wit.

"I promise it will be one for the books." Leo points to the screen displaying the anatomy of Mr. McMann. On command, everyone faces the image, and assumes a position of concerned waiting, arms folded on their chests. When the image of the patient's abdomen appears, eyebrows go up, gasps escapes into the air, and faces grimace from imaginable pain and discomfort. A large, white, phallic shape is seen occupying the length of the patient's abdomen, all the way from the anus to the diaphragm. It would seem impossible that something so large could fit into a human body. If someone had told me they had witnessed it, I wouldn't have believed them without seeing it myself. Dr. Grim orders his two residents to prep OR stat, as he goes over the images with Leo.

"This thing is huge. It is up to his diaphragm, and it has possibly traumatized the liver. The stretch from the dildo is most likely preventing a hemorrhage."

"Unbelievable!" Leo breathes out.

"Dr. Renner, Dr. Roth—I will update you after surgery; this one is certainly for the annals," quips Dr. Grim. He leaves the nurses station shaking his head, and I think I hear a quiet "ho-ho-ho". I am left wondering if it was a nervous chuckle brought on by the expectation of a complicated surgery, or a sarcastic laugh at the expense of a patient in a terrible predicament.

"You have been awfully quiet, Dr. Roth." Leo turns and addresses me.

"I think I am in slight shock at how he managed to put it up so far," I admit.

"It certainly adds to your differential diagnosis for people with shortness of breath," Leo jokes. He laughs contagiously, throwing his head back, but his laughter stops suddenly when we hear an overhead for code blue to the Ms. Leola's room. We race to the patient's room; my mind dashing through all the possible reasons for the patient to code. Did I miss something? It is my first code: do I know what to do? My palms start to sweat and my heart pounds against my chest. I feel ringing in my ears from the anxiety.

Dr. Patel has already started chest compressions when we get there. For each code, there is a sealed crash cart that gets wheeled into the room. It is packed with life-saving medications. A designated nurse stands guard, dispensing and recording the medications taken out of the cart. A team of nurses quietly performs the well-choreographed movements of bagging and pushing medications through the IV, and placing defibrillator pads on a still and limp patient. Although there are five people in the small area—not counting myself and Leo—everyone moves effortlessly...avoiding the obstacles of wires, medicine cart, and able bodies. Only one nurse stays perfectly still beside the crash cart, awaiting orders.

"Dr. Patel: why are you caressing the patient?" Leo shouts. "If you want to have any effect on her heart, I need three to four inch compressions. Do we have an airway?"

"Not yet; anesthesia should be here any minute," Dr. Patel struggles to reply as he tries to put more force into his chest compressions.

"Dr. Patel—you at least have to try!" Leo scolds the cautious Dr. Patel. He then tilts the patient's chin up, opens her mouth, and places the laryngoscope inside to lift open the airway. Leo glides in the endotracheal tube with such ease that anyone would doubt it was a difficult airway. "You have to lift up the lower jaw to see the airway. Pull the scope up, otherwise you might break the patient's teeth. They will not be happy, if you manage to save their life." Leo teaches, even under stress. "Dr. Patel: switch to bag, and Dr. Roth, start compressing."

I place my hands on the patient's chest and put all of my weight into my arms. I compress deeply, firmly: one, two, three. I start to feel her ribs give out and soften—her chest produces a sound like wet rain boots in deep mud. *This is OK; this is normal.* I calm myself, pacing my compressions. We run the code for thirty minutes: hammering compressions, delivering defibrillations, pouring medications into the body to try and start the heart. However, all of our efforts fail as this woman succumbs to the verdict of death. I am out of breath, hot, and the back of my scrubs is soaked from perspiration. This code was like running an exhausting marathon with no finish line in sight to satisfy the mind. I take my hands off the patient; we stare for the last time at the defibrillator monitor. The pulsations produced by my compressions die down and Leo announces the time of death. I catch him holding his gaze on me. Gosh, is my mind really playing tricks on me? A person just died, and I am thinking about a guy liking me. *Calm down, Mila, and don't look at him.*

I have to turn away to conceal my uncontrollable blushing, so embarrassed am I by my selfish thoughts. Leo thanks everyone and walks out of the room. The nurses are left to clean up the mess of our resuscitative efforts. Dr. Patel proceeds to type up the notes, and I am left to process the first death of my residency. A clear thought is formed and floats in my mind: a person just died, but I am failing to find a feeling of sadness, or the desire to cry. I'm left with nothing but emptiness.

"How are you holding up?" I hear Leo's voice behind me as I walk to the nurses station. There is warmth in his tone that I am happy to hear again. For a brief moment, I feel the desire to wrap my hands around him and press my head into his firm chest. But I cannot have thoughts like that…not about Leo.

"I am fine, I think. Is this normal? I mean, I feel like I should feel something, but there is nothing at all," I admit to him.

"There is no 'normal' when you practice medicine. If you processed everything like an ordinary person, you would go crazy; you would have a meltdown on a daily basis. The 'nothing' you are feeling is your protective mechanism—it helps you deal with death and illness, and whatever other bullshit you may encounter in the hospital. So, I would advise you to embrace it." He punctuates his last word with a loud stamp of the pen on the counter and then looks up at me. I don't know what it is, but when his gaze meets my concerned eyes, it softens. He gives me an apologetic smile. "I am sorry, Mila; I can be an inconsiderate brute sometimes. My honesty is not always well received, but I do mean well. Let me buy you a cup of coffee." He pauses, possibly wondering if the offer goes beyond my definition of a professional relationship. "I think our cafeteria has about ten flavors you can pick from."

"Thanks, I appreciate the offer. I can buy my own coffee, but I am actually starving. Do you mind if I get something to eat first?" I say, and I feel my stomach rumble from the nerves of the day.

"Don't mind at all...But I would suggest avoiding the cafeteria food. There is a food cart that should be parked by the entrance, and they have the best tacos in town."

Leo walks with me outside. I say to myself that this is just a lunch between two coworkers. We can eat together; this is not a date in any way, shape, or form. The July sun lifts my spirits, and for a brief moment, I close my eyes, letting the sunlight warm me up and melt the greyness and coldness of the hospital. We stand silently in a line of about five people, all waiting to order their Mexican food from the truck. The tacos turn out to be the best I have ever tried. I take a bite as soon as the basket is in my hands. The Spanish music bursting through the speakers of the food truck adds a bit of festivity to our lunch, and amplifies the flavor of the tacos.

"Aren't they good?" Leo asks when we step aside from the window of the truck. The space is limited on the sidewalk by the hospital. Some people walk inside the hospital, some sit directly on the steps of the entrance, and some lean against the wall of the building.

"Good? They are amazing!" I admit with a mouth full of taco.

"You did pretty well this morning, but my suggestion is: do not make your life about just this." He motions back to the hospital. "Over half of physicians wouldn't choose the same profession if given a second chance. Make sure that you are happy outside of the hospital, and not just when you are here. The hospital life will often disappoint you."

"Are you disappointed?"

He throws his head back and gives a loud laugh. "No, but I have low expectations of people and places."

"Isn't it unfair to yourself and others to do that?" I question him.

"Nobody says it is fair, but it is a pleasure to see a bright person like you amongst the disappointments."

"Don't do that." The compliment makes me feel uncomfortable.

"What?"

"Praise me like that. I am just like any other resident."

Leo reaches over to put a rebellious strand of hair behind my ear, but stops just as his hand nears my face, and puts it away in his pocket.

"Mila, there is something so extraordinary about you. I don't know if it is your innocence or just your positive outlook on people and life, but don't sell yourself short. I wish I had an opportunity to get to know you better, outside of this hospital, but I understand a relationship between you and I would be quite scandalous, and prone to gossip…I wouldn't want to subject you to that." He looks at me with sadness in his eyes and all I can do is just look away, because I don't want him to see how much I like him. We finish the rest of our tacos in silence. Leo's words still fill the air around us. When we return to the ER, the day goes by faster and my patients are easier to handle. Leo and I continue to chat between seeing the sick and the injured, with him finding moments to pass on to me the knowledge of practicing medicine.

When seven o'clock hits, we are almost done with the sign out to the next shift. I feel elated and pumped with energy as if I had consumed a large coffee with two extra espresso shots. Leo and I walk out together to the parking garage. We take the elevator up; it is full of other people leaving their loved ones behind, or running away from their shift. I wish the elevator didn't move so fast. I don't want to say goodbye to Leo just yet. We walk through the plexiglass tunnel with the crowd, and the humidity greets us as soon as we enter the garage. I spot Michelle a few feet away, waiting by her car. I wave back and turn to Leo.

"Nice work today, Mila," he says.

"Thank you for all your help," I say, enjoying his proximity in the vastness of the garage.

His honey-colored eyes glisten; I feel he wants to say more, but only a "see you tomorrow" escapes his lips. Leo waves to Michelle, then turns sharply on his heels and walks off without looking back.

"Giiirrrrl!" Michelle rolls, singing as she comes up close to me. "You need someone to smack that lusting look off of your face. I am your friend and as your friend, I am telling you to stay away from that fool." She wags her finger at my face with the look of a concerned mother.

"You know him?" I walk around to the passenger side of the car.

"Do I know him? Every female in our ER knows him. That man is nothing but trouble. I admit he is handsome, but there is nothing good that follows him and unless you want all the scorned nurses to start hating you, you better not show any interest in Dr. Renner." She softens when she sees my quiet discontent as a result of her warning. She opens the door and gets inside. "You have to understand something about hospital life…It is a rumor mill that can grind you into dust if you are not careful."

"He is my attempted Mr. Bangmerightnow from yesterday," I admit to my friend quietly, just in case the garage walls have ears. I get into the car. Michelle's eyes grow big and round, and her lips pucker up as she pauses after my surprising revelation. "He was nice today; I asked him to keep it professional between us," I confide to her.

I don't want to reveal to Michelle the attraction I feel towards Leo. It will be easier for me to get over him if I don't tell her that I ever liked him; at least, that's what I tell myself.

"Oh Mila, he is nice all right—nice at screwing with girls and leaving them brokenhearted." Michelle sounds off at my disclosure and starts the car.

"You know me...I don't believe in falling for a guy; I will certainly not be the cliché of a resident falling for an attending," I try to reassure my friend.

"I don't know, Mila. I don't like that look in your eyes." Michelle squints as if trying to peer into my thoughts. We drive out of the garage; it is evening, but it is still light out. The air conditioning blasts out cold air and it feels good on my skin.

"What look?"

"Horny," Michelle blurts, not taking her eyes off the road.

"Oh, shut up. I don't have that look!" I roll my eyes, dismissing her accusation. I press my head against the headrest and close my eyes. The day's events run through my head and the new emotions are processed. I hear the cars passing by, the crowds of people all joining in the orchestra of city sounds; it lulls me, and I drift off to sleep.

"Wakey, wakey sleepy head. We are home." Michelle nudges me from the unexpected nap. I groan and drag my body out of the car.

"We have to walk?" I complain, realizing that Michelle had to park a whole two blocks from our building.

"It is Brooklyn, baby."

"Fagetaboutit." I wave off my friend and shlep behind her. By the time we get home, change and eat, I am overcome with exhaustion. I drag my body to bed, but sleep doesn't take me and I decide to pick up the letters.

November 23, 1941

Iskra, you are like a star to me. You are so far away and yet you provide the light in the darkness of the night, guiding me with your love. Last night, after I came out from the hospital where air was filled with death and rotting flesh, the cold air of November hit me in the face, reaching seemingly into the depth of my brain, clearing all the thoughts except the one that we are so alone in the magnitude of the universe. I felt a deep sense of loneliness, so sharp that I felt if I were to disappear, no one would really care. I have left no meaningful imprint to be remembered by. I am sorry, but at that moment, I despaired.

The troops are slowly pushing forward. Sometimes they successfully march a few kilometers only to get pushed back deeper than they were before. Your letters bring me immeasurable joy and at the same time break my heart with your suffering. If only I could, I would feed you from my own hands...Warm your slender hands with my breath and cover your body in a blanket of kisses.

I have received a letter from Odessa. It was written by my parents' neighbor, Nikolai. It seems that at the age of twenty-four, I am an orphan. There is nobody left of my family. As I write you this I cannot comprehend how this can be true. Just six months ago, Masha, my younger sister, finished her second year of medical school. You know she was an excellent student, never anything below a five. Misha just finished high school. I was worried he would run away and join the Partisans. And little Dasha, she would always run to me so I would throw her high into the air and she would squeal with excitement. They are all gone. My parents - gone. Nikolai wrote that the Nazis just pulled all the Jews from the building; young, old, men, women and children, lined them up and shot them. Then they pulled all their belongings from their flats, separating any valuables and burning the rest. Nikolai was able to save my medical diploma and our family picture from the pile. That is all I have left of my family.

There will be no winners in this war. We all will lose something or somebody. Please stay strong. I will come back to you. You will not lose me. My heart is yours, always. Jacob.

P.S. I am sending you what is left: my diploma and a picture of my family. I think it will be safer with you.

~

December 14th, 1941

Jacob my love,

I hope this letter finds you well and in good health. The postal service is no longer working. I was lucky to have received your letter from November 23rd. I won't be able to send or receive any correspondence from now on, but I will write as promised. The writing helps me feel you are closer to me. I don't know if you will ever be able to read this. I only hope it reaches you when you have the strength to hear my news.

I never thought how emptiness can be so devastating. The whole of Leningrad, once so lively, is an abyss of noise, of life, of people. Only air raid sirens disrupt the silence. People are void of feelings or any distinguishing appearance. I often cannot tell if it is a man or a woman whom I meet in the street. We all look the same in layers of clothing—just bodies trying to survive.

In truth, I have avoided writing you. I couldn't bring myself to give the terrible news and add to the grief from losing your family. But the loss is too heavy for me to bear alone, so I ask you to bear it with me.

I received my food stamps on the first of November and I was almost home. I unlocked the door to the apartment and Dar was already putting his wet nose into my palm. He was so skinny and barely moved, but he always met me by the door. I didn't hear the noise behind me when I was pushed to the ground and a young kid, he must have been fourteen-fifteen years of age, demanded my food stamps. It was pointless to scream—no one would come to save me because they were either dead or lacked the strength to help me. He saw the determination in my eyes that I wouldn't give up my only source of survival without struggle. He pulled out a knife. In an instant Dar attacked. He found the strength to grab the boy by the sleeve. I don't think he even bit through the clothing, but the boy just stabbed him and ran off. My poor Dar laid beside me. I begged him not to leave me, but he had no fight left in him. I shrieked and I screamed like a mad woman who'd lost her child. It took me hours to wrap him in an old blanket and bring him downstairs. I sobbed, gasped for air and thought I would lose consciousness, I am so weakened by starvation. The ground was too frozen to dig, so I buried him in the rubble of the basement of the building around the corner. Aunt Olya said that I was a fool for burying him…that we should have eaten him. But I couldn't bring myself to even think of such a fate for Dar. This war has taken away everything. I cannot imagine if there will be a future where I will laugh again or feel love again. There are only memories of feelings and emotions that are left, but no strength to believe that they are to be again.

P.S. The night Dar was killed, I laid still in my bed. Any stir will cause the heat and strength to escape me. I got angry at myself for being so noble, for burying Dar. I needed to survive and Dar was the means to prolong my and Aunt Olya's life. I felt we were thieves in the night, robbing the grave, but the instinct to survive whispered that we had the right to do it. I decided that I cannot feel; feelings will be the death of the weak. I am strong. I will survive, and I will worry about the feelings later. I wanted to be truthful with you. I hope you don't judge me harshly.

I fall back into the softness of my pillow, thankful for the conveniences and comforts of the modern, peaceful day. My eyes grow heavy and I fall asleep with thoughts about my first day humming like a lullaby in my mind.

CHAPTER 10

I am looking for something in the ER supply room. The door to the room opens up and in walks Leo. I acknowledge him with a slight nod. I turn back to my search, but goose bumps erupt on my neck. I sense his gaze. He walks up behind me to reach for something off the top shelf. His breath is on my neck, which makes me flood with a warm shiver. I turn around and our proximity reveals his smell. He radiates of warmth, citrus, and fresh mint. I look up and meet his gaze of fire. It engulfs me, envelops me, and I am lifted to meet his lips. They are soft and warm. Leo slips his arm around my waist and draws me closer, the other hand glides over my neck, with his fingers slipping through my hair, cradling my head in his large palm. The kiss starts slowly, with our lips just softly touching each other, but soon caution evaporates as the intensity burns through into ash, and Leo's tongue invades my mouth, hot and yearning. The desire singes and escapes through my skin as raw heat and I wake up, in the middle of the night, sweating, with the dreamy smell of Leo still in the air.

Next morning, we round with Dr. Kramer, a balding man in his late forties with a roundness present in all his features. His face is plump and his belly the size of a late pregnancy; even his glasses are void of any angularities and his bowtie is filled with small, colorful circles. He compensates for the absence of sharp angles in his appearance by having the prickliest of personalities.

"Ah, Dr. Roth! How nice of you to finally join us." He shames me even though I am a few minutes early. "Let me make something clear to you." He looks at me and Dr. Bryce, who is a second-year resident, from under his spectacles. "I need everyone to be here by 6:45 for my shift. You are here to make my life easier. I expect not to be bothered with nuisances. You do the scud work and I will make the final decision. Is that clear? Dr. Bryce, this is your second year in this institution: I expect you to teach Dr. Roth about my work expectations." Dr. Bryce, gives a nervous nod, avoiding looking directly at Dr. Kramer. She is much taller than Dr. Kramer, but her downward gaze in his presence and anxious nodding of her head makes her appear small and unimportant. She doesn't wear any make-up, and her eyebrows are overdue for waxing. The scrubs and white coat are wrinkled, as if she has been sleeping in them. Her dark brown hair is pulled back into a messy bun. Dr. Kramer gives us a sweeping look to make sure his words have sunk in and when he is satisfied that his instructions are clear, he then proceeds. "Well, all right then. I am glad we are all on the same page."

We sit through the sign out that thankfully ends up being brief due to a slow night. I then start my shift, noticing that Leo is nowhere to be seen. I am curious to know why he is not here as scheduled, but afraid to ask anybody about his absence. I don't want to draw any attention to my interest in him, and so I just proceed with the day, hoping that he will come in later. My patients seem to present with symptoms that have a straightforward diagnosis. I have no trouble coming up with the treatment, but Dr. Kramer finds something unsatisfactory in each case.

"Dr. Roth, you didn't initiate the treatment in room three," he says, although when the case was presented to him thirty minutes earlier, he seemed to agree with the plan.

"I thought you would put in the orders, Dr. Kramer." I try to defend myself. After all, this is what he told me.

"Don't think so much, Dr. Roth. I need you to make sure things are getting done, and so far, you are failing in such a simple task."

"Dr. Roth—you are taking too long to obtain the history," he announces when I spend just twenty minutes with a seventy-five-year-old male suffering from diabetes, kidney failure, and hypertension, and who presented with complaints of abdominal pain.

"Dr. Roth: why is this patient talking to me?" He turns to me, puzzled, ignoring the patient's question as to what might be causing his backache.

"Dr. Roth, where are the nurses?"

"Dr. Roth—what am I supposed to do with this?" he questions when I give him an ECG of the patient who complains of chest pain. I look at him, puzzled, and when I don't provide an answer quickly enough to satisfy his inquiry, he throws the paper at me. I catch it before it falls on the floor. I am so enraged by his preposterous behavior that my voice trembles when I try to speak.

"I need you to look at it and confirm that there are no abnormalities, Dr. Kramer. His cardiac enzymes are normal; I think he just had a panic attack and I would like for him to go home," I say with exasperation.

"Easy tiger, no need to bite. Give me the ECG," he says with unpleasant sweetness as he takes it out of my hands. "Hmm, hmmm." He pores over the patient's cardiac activity, and the results of his blood work. "Yep, you are right...He can go." I am surprised by his acceptance of my diagnosis, but don't show it. I want to avoid giving the man any satisfaction around producing emotions from me. I type up the discharge notes and walk to the other side of the ER where I find Michelle performing an ultrasound on a pregnant patient.

The woman's big belly is smooth and shiny from the growing life within it. The room is filled with the fast and rhythmic lub-dub sound of the tiny heart. The baby is active on the ultrasound, performing movements of the Irish river dance and throwing the occasional fist pump. All these movements create waves and temporary hills on his mother's abdomen. Michelle reassures the mother that she sees nothing of concern on the ultrasound, and that once the attending looks over her notes, she will be discharged.

"What's up? Is everything OK?" Michelle questions my unusual presence on her side of the ED when she walks out of the patient's room.

"Dr. Kramer is killing me today...I want to punch him and then run away and just sit in silence without anyone asking any questions." I vent, and tilt my head back slightly to prevent shedding a tear.

"That old jerk loves to torture all newbies; don't let him step all over you. Once you push back, he will leave you alone. And don't you dare cry over whatever grief he gives you—he is not worth it."

"OK. I guess I will go back and let him know I am not to be messed with. Wish me luck." I rub my teary eyes.

I hesitate to walk away, wanting to ask her if she knows anything about Leo's absence. Fear of Michelle's scolding stops me, but either my friend is very keen on reading body language, or I am bad at hiding my true intentions: my reticence fails to escape her attention.

"What is it?" she whispers, coming closer.

"Umm…Do you know if Dr. Renner is coming to work today?" I avoid looking at Michelle's face and pick at mark on the wall, trying to dig a hole there instead of under myself.

"Why do you ask?" My friend presses me for the true reason for my desire to see him.

"He was planning to bring me some articles regarding the cases we saw yesterday," I lie. "I need them, you know…I didn't realize how much I need them. I would learn a lot from them."

"Who are you talking about? I am confused. The articles, or Dr. Renner?"

"The articles of course!" I say in such a high-pitched voice that even I am surprised at how fake I sound. I clear my throat, and compose myself before I calmly say: "I just need the articles."

"I heard one of the nurses say that he took a personal day, but I don't know why." She shares this information unwillingly, adding a sigh and a shake of her head.

"I guess I can wait until tomorrow. I need to head back now, otherwise Dr. Kramer will be lost with no one to answer his questions," I say with a smirk.

"Hang in there." My friend sends me off with a light squeeze of my shoulder. "Don't wait for me tonight. I am spending the night at Rob's," Michelle shouts as I leave her to return to the unpleasantness of Dr. Kramer.

"Where have you been? Do you think this is some sort of 'come and go as you please' place?" An angry Dr. Kramer bombards me the moment he sees me.

"Dr. Kramer, I was just a few steps away. Despite your low opinion of me, I don't take this job lightly, and if you need me, please page me regarding any work-related issues." I stress the last couple of words to deter this man from asking his nuisance questions. My firmness is met by silence, furrowed eyebrows, and flared nostrils. He doesn't need to utter a sound in order to make his anger towards me more audible or palpable. My words render him speechless, but only for a few seconds.

"Your next patient is waiting for you; I expect a presentation with a plan of action in ten minutes." He walks away, leaving me in a slight shock over my own courage, which I hope will not result in more scud work.

My next patient is a man forty-five years of age, but he looks much older because of his bushy, dirty beard, and the large mop of hair sticking out from under his too-warm-for-the-season hat. Rags and layers of clothing cover his body, making it difficult to judge his weight. The nurse warns me that he doesn't want to get undressed, fearing that his clothing will be stolen. An unpleasant odor precedes his unpleasant appearance. I try to breathe through my mouth to avoid nausea as I take his history, and attempt a physical exam.

"Mr. Saymor—you said that you are experiencing abdominal pain. Can you try to be more specific?"

"My stomach hurts," he mumbles, avoiding eye contact.

"Well, can I examine you, so I can help you?"

"I don't want to get undressed. I don't want to lose my clothes." He wraps his arms over his chest.

"I will not take away your clothes, but I need to examine you. How about we make a deal? I will not make you change into a gown but in return, you will let me listen to your chest and examine your abdomen."

I am given a grunt in agreement and a slight nod to my proposition. I start the exam with the head, moving slowly through the eyes, ears, and throat. I listen to clear heart, and lung sounds. His body is thin; grayish skin stretches over his protruding ribs and spine. I ask him to lie down so I can examine his abdomen. He follows my commands, silently. Still fighting the nauseating body odor, I poke, prod, and listen.

"What are you doing?" I am interrupted by the rude intrusion of Dr. Kramer. I excuse myself and leave the room to face my least favorite person in the whole ED.

"I was examining the patient, Dr. Kramer."

"This guy is obviously looking for a bed to stay in, and a meal. Open your eyes, Dr. Roth! He is homeless! He knows what to complain about, which diagnosis will keep him here longer. He will make you order tests upon tests and he won't even have insurance! Who is going to pay for all of these tests?! You?! I want him out of my ED!"

"But Dr. Kramer..."

"Out!"

Before I can object any further, Dr. Kramer storms off, leaving me alone to deal with Mr. Saymor. I go back into the exam room and extend my apologies. It is hard to believe that this man is here for a bed and a meal. Usually there are cases like that during winter time, but now that it is summer, there is no worry of freezing to death. Doubting the logic of Dr. Kramer, I decide to disobey him and order a CT scan. I take the patient to the CT room myself. In the hallway I stumble upon Dr. Bryce who looks as exhausted as I feel; both of us are suffering from Dr. Kramer's constantly overbearing, passive/aggressive behavior.

"Where are you going, Dr. Roth?"

"CT room." I am straightforward with her as to my intentions concerning this patient.

"Is Dr. Kramer aware?" She squints at me, as if suspecting trouble.

"I placed the order; I didn't tell Dr. Kramer yet," I inform her bluntly.

"Dr. Roth, as your superior, I will give you a piece of advice: you don't want to piss off Dr. Kramer. He will make us all pay for your initiative. You better be damn sure that this CT is necessary," she whispers to me, but somehow this advice doesn't sound well meaning.

"I am an MD, Dr. Bryce, just as you are. The patient's well-being is my main priority. Dr. Kramer can yell all he wants: he doesn't scare me." I actually feel quite the opposite, but I would only admit it to myself, never out loud. Dr. Bryce hisses, and walks off to the emergency room.

Luckily, there are no emergency cases that need a CT scan and my patient is taken right away. I go into the dim viewing room and as the image is being uploaded on the screens, Dr. Kramer storms in, probably tipped off by Dr. Bryce.

"Dr. Roth, explain yourself!!! What did I tell you?!" he screeches, turning red as if his bowtie is cutting all circulation to his head.

"Dr. Kramer, please! I don't believe this patient is here for a nap. Can we just wait for the CT results?"

"You *believe*?! You *believe*?!" His rage fills the small viewing room. "Who do you think you are?! I have fifteen years of experience, and you are some first-year resident! Remember your place, Dr. Roth…It will do you some good!"

His screaming is interrupted by the radiologist, who up until now, has remained invisible in the dim lights of the room.

"Take a look at this, guys." He points to the image of the patient's abdomen. It reveals a dissecting aortic aneurysm.

I stare at the floor so that my smug expression doesn't irritate Dr. Kramer any further. He makes the tiniest of foot stomps and turns around, huffing, to make a call to surgery.

"Dr. Roth—don't you have anything else to do?" he yells, walking away, and I take the opportunity to run out of that small room, trying to contain my desire to start skipping. For the remainder of the day, Dr. Kramer is guarded by Dr. Bryce, who has been instructed to supervise all of my cases; only Dr. Bryce has been given permission to approach Dr. Kramer. This arrangement doesn't make Dr. Bryce very happy. For the rest of the shift, I feel the gaze of Dr. Bryce upon me, trying to incinerate me into the ground. By the end of the shift, I feel exhausted and worn out from the tension. I run out of the ER, fearing that Dr. Kramer might just chase me if I am too slow to leave. When I step outside, the fresh air fills my lungs and elates my tired body. I put in my headphones and blast a song proclaiming everyone to be champions, and that's exactly how I feel. I walk down mostly empty streets bopping my head to the music. The stores are already closed and hole in the wall restaurants are waiting for a rush of orders to be delivered to people with voracious appetites who came home to empty fridges.

The subway is a few blocks away, and I am not rushing to catch the train. I am enjoying window shopping when I get the feeling I am being followed. I speed up my walk when I glimpse the reflection of a tall figure behind me. He wears a baseball hat and I can't make out his face. Before I am able to run, the stranger catches up to me and grasps my hand. I try to fight off his firm hold which proves to be pointless. I see people staring, but everyone continues on, passing me by. I realize no one will help me. I then press my heel into his foot. He falls to the ground and releases my arm. I lose the headphones and before I am able to put some distance between us, I hear the man call out my name through his pain.

"Leo?"

"Who did you think it was?" he says through clenched teeth. "I called your name, but you just kept going."

"I am so sorry! I had my music on and didn't hear you at all. I thought…Oh my gosh—I don't know what I thought." I try to help him to his feet.

"I will try to avoid you late at night," he says with a chuckle.

"Why are you following me like that? You scared me." I blame him for his painful misfortune.

"I'm sorry. I didn't mean to scare you, but I wasn't able to come in to work today and I wanted to speak to you," he manages to explain through still clenched teeth.

"Oh!" I suddenly feel guilty for causing this man's pain. "Is everything OK at home?"

"Yeah, yeah…just minor troubles; it's all taken care of." Leo takes a deep breath before he stands up straight. When he tries to take his first step, it is evident that my heel has caused some damage and will result in a temporary limp.

I bite my lip and mouth another: "I am sorry."

"Don't worry—you are forgiven. How did you survive Dr. Kramer today?" He smiles, changing the topic of conversation.

I roll my eyes and sigh. "Barely…He is exhausting. He made me persona non-grata in his presence."

"Wow—what did you do to piss him off that much?"

"Just stood up for myself, I guess." I shrug my shoulders.

He laughs, throwing his head back. "Mila, you are something." We walk in silence for the next few minutes towards my subway stop. The street lights turn on, and the day crowds are gone, but the road is jammed with traffic, loud with horns and the yelling of frustrated drivers. Leo starts with slight hesitation in his voice, "If you are not too exhausted, let me take you out for a cup of coffee. You can pay for yours, of course, and I will pay for mine." He suggests this as if anticipating my objection. I smile and nod.

"There is a place a few blocks down that makes a decent cappuccino in the neighborhood."

"Sure," I agree cautiously, not knowing what he wants to talk about. We begin our stroll looking at the ground, silent, hands in our pockets.

"So, what is your story? Why did you become a doctor?"

"Why did you choose to become a doctor?" We both start speaking at once. Our sudden attempt at conversation is so cumbersome that it deserves nothing but a laugh. The laugh breaks the tension, and all of a sudden, the conversation starts to flow like music, with comfortable pauses, questions, answers and explanations.

"I don't really have an interesting story. I feel like I always was on a path leading to medicine; I can't imagine doing anything else," I admit.

"What about you? You seem to be so disappointed in what you are doing..." I ask.

He grins at my question, but his eyes don't light up, revealing an on-point assumption as to his feelings. He looks up into the sky—pausing—maybe searching for the right words to pull from the universe.

"I am disappointed...But I still love what I do. When I started, I was just like you: filled with the romantic notion of making this world better—helping people—but then you find out that most of the time, your efforts are not appreciated; you have to jump through hoops to deliver care to people. Insurances dictate which medicines you can prescribe; patients come demanding certain treatments. They trust search engines and their neighbor more than the physician in front of them. You deal with family members who do not respect a patient's will. The nursing homes frustrate with the level of abandonment." We pass by a short Hispanic man sweeping the pavement in front of his bodega. He stops what he's doing and grins at Leo and I.

"Hi, Dr. Leo! Coming for churros?" he inquires.

"Not tonight, Carlos—thanks. By the way, this is Mila; I will bring her in for churros next time." He waves to the man, smiles back and points to me.

"OK, Dr. Leo. Have a good night, Ms. Mila." He waves goodbye and returns to sweeping.

"Bye Carlos!" I reciprocate.

"It is that bad, huh? The job, I mean." I return to our conversation.

Leo just shrugs his shoulders. "I was never a happy-go-lucky person…maybe it is just my whole outlook on life. I promise that after we have coffee, I will cheer up." He nudges me with his shoulder and for the moment, he looks young and careless. A pleasant voice singing an unfamiliar song reaches my ears, I turn my head in the direction of the sound. A young man is standing on the corner belting out the tune. An empty tin can stands in front of him. Leo pauses, reaches into his pocket and throws a ten-dollar bill into the can. The young man stops singing, checks out the can, and looks back up at us.

"Thanks, doc."

"I want to hear you play that guitar, Jeremy."

"I almost have enough money, man."

"I better get front row tickets to your show when you get famous," Leo replies lightheartedly.

"You know you wiiiiiill…" Jeremy sings.

We continue walking, with Leo keeping his head down. "Do you know everyone on this street?" I inquire.

"No, just those two," he chuckles. "They were patients of mine at one time or another; they are nice people." The unpretentious revelations make Leo more endearing to me. "Here is the coffee shop." Leo opens the door for me, and the smell of coffee, warm milk, and banana bread welcomes us.

We stop at the counter; I place an order for a decaf cappuccino. The clerk looks at Leo, but I interrupt. "We will pay separately." She nods, processes my payment and then takes Leo's order of double shot espresso. He pays, and then with a slight, quick touch of my waist, leads me to the seat by the window with a small, round table and low, plush armchairs. I sink my body into it and feel my muscles relax after the long day of being on alert. Leo sits down opposite me and finally takes off his baseball hat. His hair is the color of golden sand, today not controlled by gel. I imagine how it would feel to run my hands through it, pull his head back, and lean in to taste his lips. His eyes reflect the candlelight, reminding me of something so familiar, but my mind can't find the exact memory of seeing them somewhere else. His stare is so far-reaching, that I look away, fearing that it will reveal how much I like him.

The corner of Leo's mouth goes up in a warm smile; he squints his eyes slightly, and I blush at the expectation of him revealing something intimate.

"Mila—I have to be honest with you. I hope I don't scare you by being so forward, but I have learned that life is so fleeting, and that if you really want something, you have to go for it without hesitation. So, here I go: I like you. I know me being an attending and you a resident, it might appear that I am taking advantage of you, but I have dated a lot—too much probably—and I have never felt so drawn to somebody." He pauses, giving me a chance to react to his revelation.

I sit up, processing what Leo has told me and what I should say back. My heart and my mind start a battle and I don't yet know how to choose a winner. The logical assumption would be to shut down Leo's advances, to not give in to this feeling of uncontrollable attraction, this chemical reaction…But the irrational part of me, which for some reason has become very loud and obnoxious, tells me to listen and give him a chance. Is there a possibility for my heart and mind to coexist? I hope so...

"You are quiet...hmm. Say something! You can tell me to get lost; I would completely understand."

"That's the problem...I can't just tell you what I think. You are my attending: we are going to be working together for the next few years. I don't want a work relationship to define me. What if we break up? I have to think about my career that's just starting. I don't want to be a cliché." I share all my logical fears.

"I don't want you to feel afraid to say no. It will not affect our working together. These are my last few days at this hospital...I will be leaving next week for a position in Brooklyn, and then you won't have to face my pathetic ass. That is why I decided to ask if you feel the same." He raises his hopeful gaze to meet my wide-open eyes. I realize that this man has exposed his feelings to me, and his vulnerable soul awaits my judgment.

"I don't understand how you can just like me. You don't even know me." I seek explanation of Leo's attraction, but if asked to do the same I would struggle to find the reasons for it.

He shrugs his shoulders, but continues boldly. "I like your confidence. You speak with such clarity; you are smart, and sweetly naive. You are not afraid of a challenge. Your eyes...I couldn't forget them from the first day you stumbled into me. I want to be closer to you—to smell the curls of your hair, to kiss your fingers, to have you be mine. The attraction, the desire, is primal: it can't be explained. I decided to accept it, and speak to you honestly." I reach out and touch his firmly-clasped fingers. He opens them up, wrapping his large hands over mine.

"Leo, I do like you." I reveal my illogical feelings towards him. I lack any desire to hide anything from him. His shoulders relax, he leans back and I notice his chest slowly rise and fall with a sigh. The tension is released with a soft chuckle. He looks back at me and his eyes glow warmly. I smile back at this open happiness of the man who can be so collected and unemotional at work.

He quickly turns serious again; his eyebrows furrow before he proceeds. "I have to ask you for a favor. Your life as a first-year resident sucks, and I don't want to make it any more complicated." I cock my head slightly, not knowing what he is leading up to. "Please don't tell anyone at work about us. I have made some mistakes in the past, and some people don't think very highly of me, and rightfully so, but I don't want their disdain for me to be transferred onto you."

"Sure, but then I have to ask you for a favor in return."

"Anything." He nods in agreement.

"If you don't want me to say anything at work, then our relationship can only be platonic until you are no longer working with me."

"You mean, no sex?"

"No sex. I have to protect myself," I clarify.

Leo erupts in laughter, but quickly grows serious. "Wow, you're really looking ahead; here I am, worrying about the first kiss."

"I do like to live with a plan in mind. I'd rather discuss things before I get emotionally attached."

"Agreed. We will have as many platonic dates as you want...I promise there will be no pressure from me. I will do anything to make sure that you trust my intentions."

At this point, I wonder if I should tell my friend Michelle about this conversation, but soon swat that thought away, not arriving at a definitive answer.

"Why are you leaving the hospital?" I decide to pivot the conversation.

"There is no one particular reason—I just want a different perspective, new experiences. I have been in the same hospital from the start of my residency." He shrugs his shoulders. A waitress brings our coffee, mine complete with intricate outlines of hearts in the milk foam.

"Any advice on internal politics?" I take the mug into my hands and the warmth of the coffee transfers to me.

"Something tells me you will be just fine." Leo takes a long sip of his espresso. "Listen to Ms. MJ...She will take care of you, and make sure the nurses are doing their job. Dr. Kramer has always had power issues: just go to the director of residency program if he is out of line. You have yet to meet Dr. White—she is great. Learn as much as you can from her. Dr. Kim will let you do the most procedures; he is a very patient man.

"Thank you," I say and I smile at him. I bring the cup to my face, and the aroma of cappuccino hits my nose. My lips dip into the warm, airy foam. I take a delicious sip.

"Anytime. You know, you have the most beautiful smile," Leo compliments. "And now it looks delicious with that milk mustache..." He hands me a napkin.

"Thank you. I got the good smile genes from my grandmother." I wipe my lips.

"Well, judging by her granddaughter, she must be a beautiful lady."

"She was my role model," I say affectionately of a woman who was nothing short of a pillar of strength for our family.

"Then, I would like to meet her one day."

"Unfortunately, she passed away six months ago."

"I am so sorry, Mila." Leo reaches out and puts a loose strand of hair behind my ear without holding back. His hand barely touches the skin of my cheek, but the minimal contact creates an uncontrollable wave of desire within me.

"Mila, you are remarkable. You are making me feel things that I thought I was incapable of feeling. I think it is better if I get you home...You've had a long day; you need to rest."

His sudden change in tone wakes me up from my lulled state. "Get me home? How? You have a car?" I was so entranced by Leo and our conversation that I didn't realize that my cappuccino was finished; only the empty mug remained in my hand.

"I do...It is parked down the street. Come; I will introduce you."

"Introduce me? To your car?" I ask, puzzled. "Does she have feelings?"

"Yes, she can be quite temperamental," Leo responds.

"I look forward to meeting her then." We step outside. Leo takes my hand into his and we stroll just a block away from the coffee shop. The street is quiet and welcoming with brick townhomes and mature trees. The narrow, one-way road is crowded with closely parked cars.

"Is this one yours?" For some reason, I point to the teal Camaro that stands out amongst the modern lines of grey and white cars.

"This is my pain and passion; my work in progress." Leo proudly introduces me: "Meet my Z28, 1991 Camaro." As he says this, he lovingly strokes the hood. "Let's hope she behaves tonight, and doesn't get jealous of you." He gives the top a gentle pat and opens the door for me, holding my hand while I ease into unusually low seats. Only when I am settled does Leo get behind the wheel. His Camaro doesn't seem to mind me, and starts rumbling loudly at the turn of the key. The ignition lead is picked up by the car's stereo, surprisingly belting out a seventies dance song by the Swedish quartet whose songs I recently got reacquainted with in the movie starring Meryl Streep.

"You are such a dork," I say, and I burst out laughing. The powerful propulsion of the engine presses me back into the seat as Leo puts his foot on the gas.

In the dimness of the car's interior lights—periodically interrupted by the overhead streetlights—I examine Leo's face. His sharp jawline is covered in short stubble, he drives with one hand on the steering wheel, and the fingers of his other hand rub his chin, occasionally touching his full lips. Eyelashes that would make any woman jealous frame eyes that squint slightly while concentrating on the road; his thick eyebrows finally look relaxed, and his short hair is cut so precisely that it probably needs maintenance every few weeks. My secret examination is interrupted by a sudden jolting of the car.

"What the fuck is this guy doing? Are you all right?" Leo asks. He glances at me quickly, giving my leg a quick squeeze and sending a wave of electric goosebumps over my skin. The car in front of us has lit up with brake lights, even though there is nothing in front of it.

"What happened?"

"I just flashed my headlights to get him to move out of the passing lane, and he stopped dead." Leo's face hardens and he tries to move over to the other lane. The car in front of us moves over too, blocking, continuing to brake. I sink into the seat, digging my fingers into the door handle as my right foot presses an invisible brake pedal. Leo speeds up and makes another attempt to pass the car only to be blocked again, forcing him to brake firmly in order to prevent a collision.

"This guy is crazy! What is wrong with him?!" I scream. "Just let him drive off!"

Leo slows down, but the car in front of us slows down as well.

"Hold on. I am going to try and pass him," Leo says with an unwavering reassurance, not taking his eyes off the car in front of us. He gives the driver of the other car the horn, which is acknowledged by another quick stoppage. Leo takes this braking as an opportunity, and presses the Camaro's gas pedal to the floor, sending us shooting ahead with a loud roar of the engine. As we pass the other car, my eyes meet the stare of a woman behind the wheel. She looks like a young teenager, with long black hair shaved on one side. Her stare is full of rage and sends a shiver down my spine; I feel her anger is directed specifically at me. The girl gives me the finger as Leo's car puts distance between us. As we speed by, Leo shakes his head at this aggressive driver.

"New York drivers for you…Are you all right?"

"Yes—just in slight shock," I admit. "That girl looked scary."

"Huh? You said it was a girl?"

"I think so."

Leo is quiet for a few minutes, his right hand tightly gripping mine. "I am sorry about that. I didn't want to scare you. I promise I will get you home in one piece."

I just nod and give him a slight smile, desperately wanting a hug to calm my nerves.

The rest of the drive on Brooklyn-Queens Expressway is uneventful. Only a few cars are present on the road at this hour. Leo drives the car steadily, and we reach my apartment building in twenty minutes.

"Thank you for the ride."

"My pleasure." He takes my chin, forcing me to look into his eyes. "Mila, if I could I wouldn't let you go home alone, but I want to take it slow…I don't want to rush our relationship either. You are someone special, and I want to savor each moment with you."

In the pit of my stomach, the pleasure is brewing, emitting the warmest of sensations. Leo leans over and our lips meet; my desire for him boils over as his tongue enters my mouth, passionately caressing, taking over my mouth as if he were starving for my kisses. My fingers sink into the back of his hair, drawing him ever so close. He tears away from me, eyes on fire, transfixed on my mouth.

"You have to go. Get some rest…"

"Yes, you're right." I pull away, and compose myself.

He gets out of the car, walks around, and helps me out of the low seat. We walk to the entrance of my apartment building firmly holding hands.

"I think I have to leave you here because if I get any closer to your apartment, it will be more difficult for me to leave. Do your windows face this side of the street?"

"Yes—they are those two corner windows on the second floor." I point to the windows of my apartment on the building's facade.

"I will wait for you to turn on the lights before I drive off." He pulls me in towards him, lifting my chin to his lips, only now his kiss is soft, controlled, and yet so full of desire. I have to be on my toes to reach him; my body is a magnet drawn to his. Leo pulls away from the kiss but before letting go of my hand, he kisses the inside of my wrist.

"I will see you tomorrow," he whispers, and he walks away swiftly to his car, without looking back.

The elevator slowly delivers me to the second floor. My legs are heavy and soft from the long day in ED, but mostly from the unresolved climax of my desire. I walk into the quiet, hot apartment and hear the Camaro's engine roar as Leo drives away. In the emptiness of the apartment, I take off my clothes and walk around in my underwear, letting my skin release the heat while the air conditioner cools down the place.

I plug my phone in to charge when the doorbell erupts in an impatient ringing.

"You changed your mind?" I say before I peek my head through the door, hiding my almost naked body, giddy with excitement that Leo decided to come up. But my smile is erased at the sight of Max Kogan, grinning at me as he holds a bouquet of red roses and a bottle of Champagne.

"What are you doing here? And how the hell did you get my address?" I berate him.

"Aren't you going to invite me in? I came to bring my apologies for my behavior," he says, purposefully stretching out the words.

"Apology accepted. Now leave! I have a busy day tomorrow, Max. I have to go. Don't come here anymore."

I try to close the door, but Max props it open with his foot. "Listen Mila: I always get what I want, and your behavior the other day turned me on. I see you found yourself some schmuck who drives you around in shitty cars, but believe me, I will get what I want." He slowly puts down the Champagne and flowers as he lets go of the door.

"Leave me alone!" I quickly slam the door shut in disbelief. My heart is trying to jump out of my chest; my hands are trembling from the encounter. I peek through the glasshole on the door to make sure my unwelcome visitor is gone. I turn on my still-charging phone and call Michelle, but I only get her voicemail. I hang up, and decide to take a calming shower. The hot water settles my heightened nerves and relaxes my body. I drag myself to bed and decide to read the next letters between Iskra and Jacob.

Jacob, my love,

Today is December 24th. It is hard to believe that it has been two years since we met. Today, I woke up imagining how this day would go if we were still together. I dressed in my finest layers of rags. I pretended I am a gypsy with colorful layers of skirts and ruffles. I braided my hair, just the way you like it, with the long braid wrapped around my head. I was even able to master a small paper flower and placed it behind my ear. I pinched my pale cheeks to bring some color and bit my lips so they looked kissable for you. You know, I even set a table, although it was a small chair with peeling paint and there were no plates, but there were two small tin cans of peaches and tushenka - a feast. Instead of fine crystal flutes, I had one metal cup with the finest cold water in town. Our dinner would have been filling. I imagine I would have roasted a duck with apples and potatoes. There would be a fresh salad of tomatoes and cucumbers tossed in sunflower oil. We would enjoy red caviar on small pieces of buttered pumpernickel. After dinner, I would brew tea with leaves of bergamot and orange peel and we would sip it while enjoying the freshest Napoleon cake from the bakery around the corner. When I had cleared the table, you would start the patephone, come up to me from across the room, and bow slightly, reaching for my hand. As your lips touched my hand, your eyes would meet mine, sending pleasant shivers down my back. You would then lead me into a dance. I would not quite hear the music; I would place my head on your chest following the rhythm of your heart.

This is what I will be waiting for when the war is over. For now, I will have my daily allowance of grey green bread and try to fight the constant desire to fall asleep.

I am waiting for you, Jacob. Please come back to me. Loving you always, Iskra.

5 January, 1942

Iskra,

I haven't received any letters from you in the longest time. Each day without a word from you gets longer and longer. I know that Leningrad is suffering large civilian casualties. We hear constant stories of the courage of the people of Leningrad, despite the food shortage and the constant bombardment. Of course, no true suffering will be described to the troops to avoid demoralization. I just hope you are not hurt and you get enough provisions. There is nothing more I wish for than to reach out and hold you.

The other night I dreamt of you. The dream was so real, that after waking, I thought that the war is all but a nightmare. I dreamt of our last May together at my grandparents' dacha—the smell of lilac still in the air. Do you remember that? Those memories are a fleeting moment of joy and hope in the misery of daily existence.

This war brings no glory. It turns people into savages…Ones who are driven only by basic instincts of survival. Soldiers are starving—they are dirty and flea infested. Their desire to survive pushes them to commit self-harm: they shoot their left hand or foot just to be able to get away from it all. The desperate pain in their eyes haunts me every time I close mine.

Medical personnel are not doing much better… Many are starving, especially the men. I was surprised to see that Dr. Demin and the nurse Alena were not exhibiting any signs of dystrophy, and were seemingly physically well off. Dr. Demin's stories of successful hunting trips were not adding up…Where would he find the time? We are barely getting a chance to sleep, and with battle all around us, it is completely unsafe to venture out. I should have left him alone, believed his story. But my curiosity led me to follow him. I found him going down to the morgue; I checked the bodies after he left. He is eating human flesh!!! The insanity of my finding turned my insides out. I went to confront him, only to find him and Alena enjoying a meal. They invited me to join in the freshly cooked "rabbit," but once they saw the shock on my face, the offer was withdrawn with the simple explanation that they were just surviving, and they kept on eating!!!

I reported both of them…I had to. A military tribunal was swift; the morgue is now secured by guards, with the bodies lying untouched until we can bury them.

My dearest Iskra, I hope I am never driven to rationalize committing such travesty. Where my only option of survival is to eat the person next to me, I will choose death. I hope you will never have to bear witness to the ugliness of the human desire to survive at the expense of another human being's death and suffering. Wishing to hold you tight and never let you go…Sending you all my love. Yours, Jacob.

As I put down the letters, I am overcome by sadness for the suffering that my grandmother and her fiancé had to endure. The unimaginable choices they made seem gargantuan compared to my struggles. My thoughts of the day are rudely interrupted by sleep, but not before I have committed to memory the lessons that my grandmother wanted me to learn from her story.

CHAPTER 11

I am standing at the beach, small pebbles massaging my feet, and warm waves kissing the skin on my legs. I look to the horizon, longing, waiting for something, but the clear sky melts into the water, reflecting only the warm sunshine. I look down and find a yellow stone, an amber, brought by the waves right to me. The dark green and yellow specks glisten gold within a clear, light, honey-colored stone. I lift it up and look at the sun through the amber.

"That's a beautiful stone, my angel," I hear a familiar voice say from behind me.

I look back and see my grandmother, gazing straight at me, lovingly. The remembered pain of losing her, and the happiness of having her here again makes me erupt in tears.

"Don't cry, Mila. Everything will be all right." She comes closer, and wipes the tears from my eyes.

"The stone chose you; don't lose it. It will bring you great love. I know…I once had it too." She looks at the stone in my hand and closes it within her fist. Her hands are so familiar—the skin of the fingers overtaken by arthritis is warm and soft. The fire of her red hair has gone out, and has changed into the color of white snow.

The curls, as always, are neatly tucked into a small bun. She is just a bit shorter than me, a change that occurred in the past few years; I am still not used to looking down at her. She was always a person who made me look up: her enormous personality filled the room, and everyone was touched by her attention. Grandmother's dark eyes look at me now with sweet adoration.

"It is just a stone, Grandma."

"Things are just things until they find a purpose. This amber has a purpose and it is to make you happy, my angel." She places a soft kiss on my forehead and when I open my eyes, I am cuddled into my pillows and blankets, but the soreness within my chest is palpable—a reminder of the real loss still felt from the death of my grandmother.

The sound of waves emanates from my cell phone, announcing that it is 5:30 a.m. My phone alarm has performed its duty. Despite the eventful previous day and seemingly short night, I feel rested.

"Good morning, sleepy head." A message pops onto the screen from Leo.

"Good morning to you as well," I send back.

"Get ready. I will pick you up in half an hour." Leo notifies me. I quickly rush through my morning routine and meet him outside as he stands by his teal Camaro. This time, the car radio is blasting out an eighties song from a British rock band. The morning hours are pleasant, and void of humidity. The streets are empty…Most people are still asleep. Since very little traffic is present on the roads, I know it will be a quick drive to the hospital.

"You have quite a versatile taste in music," I poke fun at him and get into the car.

"I have my parents to thank for that. They had lots of parties when I was growing up, so the house was never quiet." Leo starts the engine, which roars loudly in the early morning hours.

"Where do they live?"

"My parents? On Long Island…I want to take you to meet them on Saturday. They are having a small dinner party."

"Are you sure it is not too soon?"

"I was never more sure in my life—they will love you," he replies without hesitation.

We cross from Brooklyn to Manhattan, this time without encountering any aggressive drivers.

"I will drop you off at the entrance and meet you inside for rounds."

"Yes, OK. I don't want to start any rumors." I voice my understanding of his reasoning around being discreet.

We pull up to the hospital, the sun and most New Yorkers still asleep. The hospital is far from being affected by the night's end and the beginning of the new day. The building is humming and buzzing: people are as busy as bees taking care of their hive. Everyone has a purpose, and there is an unspoken hierarchy. The bottom dwellers are represented by the nurse's aides and the patient transporters. They are directed by the nurses, who have a hierarchy of their own: one which doesn't always bow, even to the physicians. The nurses' union has granted them many protections; they are the untouchables of the hospital kingdom.

Many physicians—having suffered through their residency—bestow the torture onto their residents, who are overworked and sleep deprived, yet bear the brunt of patient care. Sure, there are regulations: guidelines dictate the number of hours residents can go without sleep, and the maximum number of hours they can work. But the king of the kingdom—profit—always hungry for revenue, demands even more from residents and they can only obey. Residents can't anonymously file complaints regarding violations; nor do they want to. If their program comes under review and is put on probation, the residents are the ones who will suffer. So, they quietly work and work, sleeping where and when they can, learning to doze off in the most uncomfortable of positions.

As I enter the hospital today, I suddenly feel the enormity of this institution's role compared to my minuscule existence in the realm of patient care. But today, I feel I can conquer all: the tough patients, the mean attendings, and the gossiping nurses. The man that I like likes me back, and today, I am a happy girl.

Michelle meets me by the nurses station. Her look of dissatisfaction puts me on alert. Silently, she hands me a cup of coffee and with a nod of the head and a roll of her eyes, she motions towards the supply closet of the ED.

"What is wrong with you?" Michelle whispers once we're in the closet.

"What do you mean? And why are we hiding, and whispering in this closet?" I whisper back.

"We are here because someone didn't listen to my warning and now all the nurses are chatting about how you are the new arm candy for our Dr. Renner."

"I am not his arm candy! We had coffee last night after my shift - that's all," I protest.

"And today, he is dropping you off in front of the hospital? He may as well have walked in with you, arm-in-arm. Did you sleep with him already?"

"Are you seriously asking me that? It is no one's business, and you should know better than that," I reprimand Michelle.

"I'm sorry, Mila—I'm just looking after you. You're book smart, but your studying didn't teach you how to deal with pettiness and gossip. Nurses can be vicious if they don't like you."

"It is all right; I can handle it."

"You know I don't trust Dr. Renner…Too many rumors floating around about him," Michelle reiterates.

"They are just rumors, Michelle. He is being straightforward with me." I try to reassure her.

Michelle gives me a penetrating look as if searching for any wavering in my determination; she finds none, and gives me a light nudge. "So…Did you sleep with him?" she quips with a smile.

"No, of course not! Are you crazy? You know me better that that!" My accusatory tone causes my friend to apologize.

"OK, OK! Pardon my curiosity!"

"Well, to give some satisfaction to your curiosity, I must inform you that I do really, really want to sleep with him." We burst out giggling and I feel relief in coming clean to my friend. Our closeted chuckles are interrupted by Ms. MJ who walks in on us and gives us a disapproving stare. She announces that the rounds are starting.

We put on our serious faces before we come out of the supply closet. Michelle goes to her side of the ED and I go in the opposite direction to join Leo for rounds. At the nurses station, I see Ms. MJ again. She is talking to a beautiful and statuesque blond who looks fresh out of a hair salon with her beautifully done hair and makeup. Only the custom embroidery on her crisp white coat—which appears freshly pressed—gives out a clue that she is Dr. White, of the emergency department.

"Dr. White? Hi, I am Dr. Roth, first-year resident." I stretch out my hand for a shake.

"Dr. Roth…Very nice to finally meet the woman who stood up to Dr. Kramer; I am impressed." She shakes my hand firmly, giving me an approving look at the same time.

I blush at hearing her praise. "News spreads fast around here, huh?"

"That kind of news does," Dr. White says warmly.

"Dr. White—are you going to be working the day shift today?" I inquire.

"No, I am going to give you your sign out. I'm done with my shift. I came in for Dr. Kim yesterday… he had some emergency business to attend to." That would explain not seeing her at the evening sign out yesterday.

I look at her, slightly puzzled. Her appearance doesn't give any hint that she has worked through the night. She doesn't wear scrubs, and there is a pleasant veil of perfume around her.

It must have been apparent that I was looking at her in bewilderment because she unexpectedly addresses my silent musings.

"ED is a miserable place; there is no beauty here. I feel I could suffocate sometimes, especially at night. There are no windows! I suspect that EDs are built this way on purpose...People who work here will not realize what time of day it is by looking through the window, and will just focus on work. I change into nice things so I can leave the ugly scrubs behind as soon as I am done. Beauty is a pathway to eternal happiness and the projector of optimism for others...I truly believe it is a building block of life. I apologize for my monologue: the night shift does this to me sometimes. Where is Dr. Renner?"

"I am here." Leo walks up, his breathing hastened from the rushed walk. "Sorry for the delay—seems as though the parking lot is unusually packed today." He stands close behind me; I try not to look back and avoid his eyes, fearing that eye contact might give away our secret attraction. His proximity tests my willpower and the ability to control my emotions—it sends my heart into a gallop that spreads warmth throughout my body.

We are joined at this moment by the second-year resident, Dr. Bryce. She exchanges quick pleasantries with everyone and we start the sign out. Dr. White manages to do it so eloquently—as if reading a poem during evening tea. Her presentation of every patient is organized and orderly; she goes through each test and study ordered with a brief explanation and the reasoning behind each one. She even manages to pepper Dr. Bryce and I with occasional questions that feel like a cheerful conversation amongst longtime friends, mixed in with light-hearted jokes. As soon as the sign out is over, Dr. White escapes the hospital walls, but reminds me that we will be working the day shift together tomorrow. This woman radiates such a regal presence that I perform a mental curtsey.

The day's monotony follows a familiar schedule: after sign out, we round on all the patients and then Dr. Bryce and I start seeing the first sick and injured of our shift. We decide to take patients as they come. Dr. Bryce keeps the conversation between us short and seems to be annoyed by my presence. I decide to ignore her attitude and concentrate on my work. I still have to report all my cases to her, and then Dr. Renner will give the final sign off. I look around ED for Leo before I walk off to my next patient. My search ends when I meet his blazing stare across the hallway...He gives me a wink and my smile stretches from ear to ear. He walks off and my eyes meet the stare of another somehow familiar person glaring at me from the other side of ER. I have seen this woman somewhere before. She is looking directly at me; her long black hair is stringy and uncombed and it sticks out from underneath a baseball hat. Her clothes hang loosely on her skinny frame. I start walking towards her, but she quickly disappears from my sight before I can reach her. I feel the unsettling worry that this woman wants something from me, but decide to dismiss it. I turn around and go to see my next patient. I start to smile to myself again, remembering the wink Leo gave me earlier.

My jovial expression quickly disappears when I see Max Kogan on the stretcher.

"What the hell are you doing here?" I manage to pronounce after the shock of this encounter makes me almost choke on my own saliva. I wonder what I did to cause fate to keep this jerk around me.

"Dr. Roth! What a pleasure to see you here. If I knew you worked here, I would have made sure I got sick more often." He stretches out both his arms, calling on me to come in for a hug as if we were friends. He licks his sausage lips in self-satisfaction. I step back from him so that he cannot reach me.

"This is not a clinic and I am a first-year resident, not your personal physician. I think it would be questionable for me to take care of you. I will have Dr. Renner come in and examine you."

"Is he the schmuck who took you home last night?"

"His name is Dr. Renner and if you have a legitimate reason to be here, I better hear it right now!" He is in my domain now. I will not let him behave like a spoiled child here.

"My heart is hurting."

"Oh, for God's sake—do you even have a heart?"

"Oh sure; I think it is somewhere in this region." He makes circular motions in his general chest area.

"Is this all a joke to you? There are people out there who need help and you are taking up valuable space and time!" I berate him.

"What can I say? My heart is hurting and I believe I am at the right place for this to be taken care of." He crosses his feet and puts his hands behind his head as if lounging in a resort and not the ED. Understanding that I will not be able to get rid of Max by shaming him, I decide to proceed with the evaluation of his complaint, hoping to pacify him and avoid drawing any of the hospital staff's attention to my now very evident stalker. He answers all my inquisitions with a small, unpleasant smile. The responses are detailed and lengthy: I think he is enjoying listening to his own voice. When Max finishes the description of his symptoms, in walks his mother. She is a plump, short woman with a stiff helmet of bright red hair that is probably done once a week. Her eye makeup is made up of bright purple eyeshadow, framed by extremely arched, tattooed eyebrows. Her lips are finished off with the most vulgar red lipstick. She greets me by placing two loud kisses on my cheeks. I don't return the gesture. I only met this woman a couple of times when visiting Mom at her job. Max's mom doesn't notice my failure to greet her in the same manner; she releases me from her hug and shakes her head, looking at her son.

"Can you believe it, Mila?! My son, the smartest man I know, is in this hole of a hospital. My personal cardiologist is coming over shortly and my Max needs to be transferred out. He is so precious; I need him to receive the best care possible. Would you be a darling and see if we can get a nicer room than this?"

"Excuse me, Mrs. Kogan, but this is an emergency room not a hotel, and I am not a concierge. Certainly, a transfer can be discussed, but since you are here, we have very capable physicians who can provide a high standard of care to your son."

As she fixes her son's perfect haircut, the red-haired woman giggles at my sternness. "Don't worry, Max... Mommy will take care of everything. Mila, you are so serious. I don't mean to offend you, but Maxi was not feeling well at breakfast today. He threw up, and my cooking is the best. I love cooking for him when he visits. I am such a clean person and everything I feed him is only organic, so I panicked! Plus, he said he was feeling so tired and he got so sweaty, I had to rush him to the nearest hospital even though this hospital never makes New York's best hospitals list. But of course, it is wonderful that you are here: Max will really need a lot of special care. At least for now, I am happy that he is in this hospital because it is close to my house." I understand that I have to now deal with both Max and his mother.

I explain to both of them that we will first order an ECG to evaluate his cardiac status, as well as blood work, and then proceed depending on the results. I leave him wallowing in self-satisfaction and try to decide how to present this to Leo. I conclude that it is better to be honest and explain how I became acquainted with the jerk. I find Leo typing notes at the nurses station. I start presenting the case as if Max were any other patient.

"Did you order an ECG?" he asks, not raising his head from the chart.

"I did."

"And?"

"Hmm…Well there is something I want you to know before we go any further."

Leo's fingers stop the fast-paced typing; he looks up at me and his eyebrows furrow with concern at my all-of-a-sudden hushed tone. I explain that the patient is the blind date my mother set me up with, and he is the one I was running away from when I stumbled into Leo a few days ago.

"I don't think you should be taking care of him. I will have Dr. Bryce take over."

"I will not withhold proper treatment just because I dislike him, but you are right." I bite my lips and nod my head.

"I know you wouldn't, but you make yourself vulnerable for malpractice when you take care of patients like that. If he ever decides to sue you, his lawyer will tear into you and make you regret you ever felt bad for him as a patient. I'll put a stop to his demands; he is not in charge here."

"Well, his mother is in charge...Plus, he saw us together last night, when you dropped me off." I play nervously with my fingers.

"It doesn't matter. I will not have anyone dictate their demands in my ER and blackmail you, or any other resident here." We are interrupted by the nurse who brings us Max's ECG strip.

"Well, what do you know—it looks like he is having ST segment changes. I better go tell him he is having a heart attack." He gives me an encouraging rub of the shoulder. "Please call in code heart," Leo instructs me as he walks off to deal with Max. I dial in and the overhead speakers announce "code heart" to the room of Max Kogan. A predetermined cardiothoracic team will race in to start interventional treatment of this unpleasant person, who probably thought himself invincible until now.

I stay out in the hallway, hoping that Max will not expose my late night rendezvous with Leo to the hospital staff. While Leo delivers the findings to Max, I keep myself busy by seeing other patients. I manage to take care of an elderly woman who I suspect is having diarrhea caused by a bacteria-clostridium difficile, and start nebulizer treatment on an asthmatic girl before I see Leo again.

"How is he?" I am curious to find out Max's reaction to his diagnosis.

"Lost for words…The diagnosis sent him into a stuttering paranoia. Turns out he is an occasional cocaine user, which would explain this early MI. The cardiologist is talking to him right now and then he is being admitted. I doubt he will have the nerve to bother you again."

"Wow. I actually feel bad for him." Max now becomes a patient; getting him better is all that matters.

"Don't bother feeling sorry for him. He will receive the best of care, despite his arrogance."

"Do you ever find it difficult to take care of people you don't like?"

"No. I don't have to be nice to them, but there is standard of care. There are protocols that I have to follow: it helps to take the emotion out of it."

"Hmm…You make it sound so easy. Isn't it ironic that doctors are expected to be compassionate, but then, at the turn of a switch, need to take emotion out of patient care, and just perform?"

"Look at you! Not even a week on the job, and you're already philosophizing about the irony in practicing medicine. Mila, as a physician who is only starting out, you are naive and eager. This job can make anyone a cynic; others, who never worked in medicine, will never understand it. They will never experience bringing a life into the world, keeping it going, and then failing to preserve it—sometimes all in one day. You will be making some tough choices in your career…you just have to make sure they are always for the benefit of the patient. Nothing else matters."

"*You* matter to me." I hold back on coming closer to him. I want to lay my head on his chest and listen to the sound of his heart, a heart which is full of care.

He looks piercingly from under his brows into my eyes; his own eyes twinkle with mischief and desire.

"Come with me," he groans.

I follow him to the supply closet and as soon as the door shuts behind me, I can no longer hold back my yearning for this man. We start to kiss, feverishly, hungry for each other's lips. He runs his fingers through my hair, cradles my head, drawing me closer. My hips press tight against his, feeling the hardness of his body.

"What are you doing to me?" he mutters under his breath, peeling away.

"It is a good thing we will not be working together." I manage to produce an out-of-breath smile, enjoying Leo's admission.

"Yes, but now we must go back to work…God, you are so beautiful." Leo cups my face and then slides his hands down my arms. Our fingers and eyes interlock, and he draws me in for one last kiss. Then, finally our lips part, but our fingers stay clenched together. The spell is broken only when we both take a step back. My fingertips slide down to Leo's palms, fingernails lightly scratching the surface of his skin and brushing along the length of his fingers. He closes his eyes as the pleasure of my touch washes over him. "You really have to go," he grunts. I nod in agreement and we walk out of the supply room, separately, but before leaving, we fill our hands with miscellaneous supplies to avoid suspicion as to the true purpose behind our both being in this room.

I immediately get busy so that my mind can suppress the desire in my heart. My next patient is a fragile, white-haired, hunchbacked man by the name of Baruch Katz. His chart clearly displays DNR/DNI, ordering no intubation or resuscitation in the event that his body gives up. Mr. Katz had activated his emergency button when he fell and couldn't get up. I evaluate his injuries, suspecting he has a fractured hip.

"You are so nice and so young…God bless all the doctors in this place." He winces as I try to move his left leg. He is eighty-six years old; his body looks small and weak without clothing. Mr. Katz's back is no longer straight so he has to have several pillows to prop up his neck. The curvature of his spine doesn't allow for him to lay flat. Each of his fingers is twisted from arthritis; his hair, the few strands that are left of it, is neatly trimmed. He tells me he still shaves every day, even though he has no particular place to be, except for doctors' visits. His pants have probably been in his possession for the last thirty years. His shirt, although clean, has permanent stains intertwined into the threading on a molecular level. His legs are bowed, and the left one is shorter and turned out—a sign that he has a hip fracture.

I proceed to make sure he has no cuts or bruises from the fall. My fingers trace over his skin—it is covered in scars from what he tells me are surgeries to remove skin cancer—and there are also many lesions:

flat and raised, in different shades of brown. I remind Mr. Katz to continue to follow up with his dermatologist and he nods. "Yes, I see one every four months." I find a small spot on his neck that I do not like, and I know it is another skin cancer. I fear he will not like me by the end of this exam.

"Cancer, shmancer. I am eighty-six years old, darling. My body is covered in scars from all these surgeries; I am just tired. Be kind to the old man."

I proceed to his right arm, then his left. The inner left forearm is stained with a tattoo - a line of numbers. I avoid touching them...I know what they mean: death, fear, pain, unimaginable loss. This old man was once a little boy, forever scarred on the inside by the small line of numbers on the outside, but only he knew the real pain of wounds he suffered during World War II.

I hear my grandmother's voice: "You have a gift and a curse. You will heal, but first you will have to learn to hear the pain, so that you will know how to take it away."

"Don't feel bad for me," the old man continues, as though reading my mind, "that pain is all but a dark shadow. I lived a happy life. I have three kids, seven grandchildren, and three great grandchildren. I will die a happy man. Let me give you a gift—I have been carrying it with me for a while, looking for the right person to give it to. Seems to me, I found her." Mr. Katz's face transforms into a huge grin as he passes me a small box. I see he wrapped it himself. I take it, noticing disheveled, tucked-in corners he has taped with various lengths of scotch tape. I give him my warmest smile.

"Thank you so much! You know, you do not have to give me anything."

He furrows his brow. "Take it. This is nothing to quarrel about. It's just a small nothing," he grumbles. I tear the paper: in the box there is a small, grey, seashell-like object. Mr. Katz quietly giggles. "Open it, open it!" His excitement warms the chill of the room.

"It's a calculator!" I declare.

"And it has a mirror!" he proclaims, as if it is the most unbelievable new-age tech gadget that has ever existed. My heart is enveloped in the warmest blanket that will forever cuddle me at the memory of this gift.

"Thank you so much. I will think of you every time I use it! Mr. Katz, is there anyone who I can contact, to let them know you are in the hospital?" I put the sweet gift away into my white coat pocket.

"No, no…I don't want to bother anyone. My three sons worry about me enough." He waves his hands vigorously in disapproval.

"I am sure they will be worried when they find out that you are not at home."

"Why would they find out? They call me several times a day to check up on me. I will just not tell them anything." He picks up a flip phone that's lying beside him, looks at the screen for a few seconds, and then puts it down.

"Don't they come to visit?"

"Of course they do…I have to swat them away. They are allowed to come visit me twice a week—no more. I still have a life you know, and they should not treat me as a child. I can still take care of myself. If my Evelyn was still alive, she would take care of me."

"How long has she been gone?"

"Almost fifteen years. She was a farmer's daughter. I met her when I was eighteen during my trip to Ireland. I married her and brought her back to America." A soft chuckle escapes his mouth at the memory of his youth. "But I go to see her every Sunday." He looks at me with the corner of his eyes to gauge my reaction, but I don't interrupt my exam while he is telling his story. I just give an acknowledging grunt that permits him to continue without being judged by me.

"I bring flowers to her grave every Sunday. Then, I sit in the car at the cemetery where she is buried and play our favorite song." He closes his eyes and hums an unfamiliar, but pleasant tune.

"Mr. Katz, this is the sweetest story I have ever heard."

"Oh, my dear Dr. Roth—you can't imagine how much I miss her, but I am forever thankful for the love she filled me with."

I finish my exam as Mr. Katz lays quietly. I pat his thin, but warm hand and explain our next step in his care. He nods in agreement and I leave him to rest. I order an X-ray of his hip to confirm my suspicions of a fracture, and a CT scan of his head to rule out any invisible trauma from the fall. Mr. Katz's story occupies my mind for the rest of the day. *Will my feelings for Leo lead to a relationship as strong as the one between Mr. Katz and his Evelyn? Does love only bestow its blessings on the select few, or are most of us just blind to love's blessings? Am I being fooled by my desire for Leo, or is it the beginning   of   something   special?*

I cannot think about all of this right now. Maybe tomorrow I will ponder the subject of Leo with a clear head. I will take each day as it comes. I will trust my heart for now, and let it lead me into the temptation of Leo's embrace.

I present Dr. Bryce with Mr. Katz's diagnosis and the care plan; she bobs her head, punctuating my every suggestion, her gaze transfixed on my eyes without blinking. I pause to ask if my presentation makes sense. She fails to produce any sound for what seems like an eternity, her gaze still drilling into me.

"You really get around," she finally barks.

"Huh?"

"Don't play stupid with me. It is your third day here, and you already think you can get your hands on Dr. Renner?"

"You know what Dr. Bryce? It is none of your business who I get my hands on, and I don't appreciate your tone." Her unexpected attack on my badly kept secret draws a surprising, but more or less professional version of the "shut your mouth or I will claw your eyes out" threat.

The usual humming of the ER is suddenly inter-rupted by a high-pitched scream that, for a moment, I doubt is even coming from a person. Intuitively, I head in the direction of the scream, leaving Dr. Bryce with her mouth half open. The hollering, it turns out, is being produced by a woman in her thirties, who is being wheeled into ED by the ambulance crew. A crowd of curious personnel swarms around the patient. Leo is assessing the screamer, asking her to lower her voice because she is making her condition worse. When

I finally get a clear view of the patient, I understand why Leo is trying to calm her down: her left eyeball is protruding from its socket. The scene reminds me of Arnold Schwarzenegger in "Total Recall" when he is suffocating on the surface of Mars. I edge through the crowd of onlookers and start speaking to the woman calmly, hoping that my attempt will distract her from producing the ear-splitting sound. My conversation with her escalates to a plea, but no one can win the battle with her voice box; attempts to reassure her are all but useless. Leo turns to me, and his eyes meet mine.

"You have to hold her down!" the request is repeated to EMTs who nod in agreement, securing the patient's flailing arms and legs. Leo swiftly injects anesthetic into the outer corner of the patient's left eye. Scalpel in hand, he makes a fast, but precise linear incision at the same spot in order to relieve constriction of the muscles around the eyeball. The shrieking stops, the patient's body relaxes, and her screams turn into sobs.

"Dr. Roth, please put a cup over this patient's eye: I don't want any pressure on it, and arrange an oculoplastic consult."

"Sure," I say, nodding.

Leo gives me a wink and a corner smile before walking off into the depths of ED; he is good at not showing his attraction. I'm now able to speak with the patient, who says her name is Lakisha. I learn that her eye suddenly popped out when she had a sneezing attack. With the help of EMTs, I guide the stretcher into one of the exam rooms as Lakisha continues talking, gesticulating vigorously to show how terrified she was of her brain coming out as well. The EMTs leave us and I explain it is impossible for her brain to just start leaking out, and that her sneezes probably just produced too much pressure, causing her eye to protrude. I finish dressing the area, and now she looks like a one-eyed cyclops, but that doesn't stop her from finding her phone and taking a few selfies before contacting friends and family to share the details of her ordeal.

I find Leo at the computer, checking lab values of today's patients. I come close and start typing my notes on the computer next to him. Due to our proximity, we can't escape the brush of our forearms. The slight touch electrifies my body.

"I like how you smell," Leo says, without lifting his head from the computer, complimenting the scent of rose water that I always spray in my hair.

"Thank you." I turn the color of a pink rose.

"I'll take you home after your shift," he notifies me. I nod and look up at Leo to see if there will be more to it than just taking me home. "I think we need to go for a walk."

"Oh."

"Oh?" he chuckles. "You don't want to go for a walk with me?"

"No, no…I do," I reassure him. I want to say what I really want him to do to me, but just give his pinky a squeeze with mine and continue to type up my notes. I feel Leo keep his gaze on me for a second, but I press my fingers hard into the keyboard and keep my head down—there is a real danger that my affection for this man may spill over and become evident to the nurses now filling up the station. Although our secret has been discovered by Dr. Bryce, I still want to avoid revealing anything to the rest of ED concerning my attraction to Leo.

"Why don't you grab something to eat? You have become so consumed by the work that you forget about your own needs." Leo cares more about me than I do. Indeed, the clock is showing 3 p.m. and I haven't acknowledged my stomach's demand for food, or my bladder's need for a bathroom break.

After a quick meal at the cafeteria, I look for Michelle on her side of the ER. One of the nurses points to the room where Michelle is examining a patient—a teenage girl who doesn't appear to be older than sixteen. I wait for my friend in the hallway just outside. She comes out a few minutes later, shaking her head from side to side and rubbing her forehead.

As she approaches me, Michelle shares the reason her young patient was in the ER. "Can you believe it? She is pregnant and she didn't even know."

"No way! Are you serious?"

"Well, there is a human being in her belly that I can see on the ultrasound, so yeah, I am serious. When I first asked her if she was sexually active, she said no. And you know why she claimed she is not sexually active?"

"No, I don't," I reply, feeling like I am being tested and should know the answer.

"Because she just laid there!" Michelle explains. I would certainly not have gotten this one correct.

"Can you please explain that logic to me?" Michelle asks, incredulous. But all I have for her in reply is a shrug of my shoulders.

"It is a vicious cycle that renders you completely helpless and hopeless," my friend continues. "Women keep having children at a younger age, they then have to work several jobs to support them, and these children— lacking the love and guidance of their parents—start having children of their own. They think that having a child will create a tight, loving family, but this dream just gets crushed by the realities of a lack of finances and total emotional unpreparedness for being a parent. Heck, I am almost twenty-five and I cannot imagine being a parent." I reassuringly rub my friend's shoulder, understanding her frustration all too well.

"Tell me about it. I remember when I was doing my rotations…We had a fourteen-year-old who came in with perianal warts. I mean, it was like a field of cauliflowers and she was insisting she was a virgin. I pressed her for more information and finally she admitted to having anal and oral sex, just not vaginal: hence her logic for still considering herself a virgin. I couldn't believe it! Her mother came in a week later, fuming about how dare we send fake bills for fake procedures on her little girl. The doc who treated her just kept repeating, 'I cannot give you any information; please speak to your daughter.'"

"I swear, teenage years make you stupid. So, this girl with all the warts had enough brain cells to have sex of various kinds, but she wasn't smart enough to give a fake home address?"

"Yep…and I have seen her in the clinic again. She shuffled in like a prisoner behind her mother. I guess she came clean because her mother was there in order for her to get birth control."

"I just don't know what is wrong with these girls—how their lives must be so screwed up to not know the difference between love and lust, and all its consequences."

"Well, I guess it's like you said: teenagers act stupidly and their brains don't keep up with their developing bodies."

"You know I will not be able to eat cauliflower for a while now," Michelle says as she wrinkles her nose.

"Oh c'mon! I didn't think work could leave an imprint on your diet."

"Oh, it does…You have no idea." My friend motions, pretending to gag with her finger inside her mouth. "I stopped drinking Coke for a long time out of cans and glass bottles because there were quite a few patients who used them up their bottoms and then couldn't get them out. Then, there was a time I couldn't even look at cottage cheese and mashed potatoes…brrrr." Michelle's body shakes with the recollection. "Doesn't it get to you?"

"No, but Dr. Bryce got to me today."

"What do you mean?"

"She accused me of sinking my claws into Leo—excuse me—*Dr. Renner*. I think that's how she put it."

"*No*, she didn't!" Michelle grabs my arm and gives it a firm squeeze.

"Oh, yes she did!"

"I remember nurses teasing her last year that she was everywhere Dr. Renner was: she took the same shifts as him, and ate lunch when and where he ate, but I don't think they ever went out. I told you it would be a mistake to go out with him. You are acting like a teenager whose brain is disconnected from their body!

Perhaps I should lecture *you* on lust and love and how to differentiate between the two."

"Stop it, Michelle! I know the difference! Maybe that is why I am choosing to date him...I feel there might be more to our relationship than just lust." Our conversation is interrupted by my pager announcing a trauma code. I leave Michelle to deal with her young, pregnant patient. I run towards trauma room where everyone is putting on blue cloth gowns and masks with shields. Leo is conversing with trauma attending; Dr. Bryce is standing by herself, and a few other residents and nurses crowd together. This scene can only mean that we have multiple traumas coming in.

As it turns out, two people with gunshot wounds are brought in by the ambulance staff. When the patients arrive, everyone intuitively knows what their role is in trauma room. Our team splits into two groups, one for each patient. Dr. Bryce helps trauma attending, and I stay with Leo. Both teams are separated by just a curtain. We help the EMTs transfer our patient onto a bed and immediately, the body of this unconscious person is swarmed with ER staff. First, Leo intubates the patient, and then respiratory tech starts pumping the airbag slowly and rhythmically to infuse the patient's lungs with oxygen. Two large bore needles are inserted into the patient's arms so that medicine and fluids can be quickly delivered into his bloodstream.

"Let's turn him over, people. I need to know how many bullet holes he has. I see one in the left mid-chest; look for the exit," Leo instructs.

The limp body of this young black, skinny, stark-naked person is rotated and checked. One bullet has traveled through the side of his chest and hasn't exited his body; another bullet has entered through the side of his thigh, exited the leg, lacerated the scrotum, and entered the abdominal cavity.

"Make sure you have a finger in every cavity! Check that there is no internal hemorrhage!" Leo guides our team.

I push in the urethral catheter which delivers non-bloody urine into the bag.

"No blood in urine," I shout. At least his bladder and kidneys are not damaged, I think to myself with relief. We turn him over and I perform a rectal exam: my glove comes out covered in blood.

"Bright red blood per rectum," I announce so that Leo can make the next decision for this patient's care.

"All right guys, step out; we need to do a chest and abdominal X-ray and then transfer him to OR," Leo announces. We all walk out of the trauma room to shield ourselves from the radiation of the X-ray. While we wait for the films to be done, Leo is approached by two tall men who introduce themselves as detectives. They inquire as to whether the patient is dead or alive, and what prognosis he has. They give Leo their business cards and ask him to update them on the outcome of the surgery. The detectives need to label this shooting as either a murder, or an assault with a deadly weapon, and this will be determined by whether our patient lives or dies.

"Let's move him, guys!" Leo summons, signaling that the X-rays are finished and the patient is ready for the OR transfer. "Stay here, Dr. Roth—see if there is any help needed with the other patient." It takes me only a few steps to peak behind the curtain, but the same organized commotion that just took place in my room is already finished. The second patient is lying still on the table with an intubation tube sticking out of his mouth. The airbag balloon has already been disconnected.

"Time of death: 6:15 p.m.," trauma attending announces, and someone records it. I come closer to the patient, who appears to be as skinny as my patient, and too young to be imagined carrying a gun. His abdomen has a vertical scar, which could mean he had already had an abdominal surgery in the past.

"We saved him eight months ago." I turn around and see Ms. MJ standing behind me, looking at the body. "He was brought here by an ambulance, gunshot to the abdomen. Our trauma surgeon really saved him. His mother was coming in once a month, thanking him for bringing her son back. It looks now like he brought him back to face the inevitable. I don't know how his mother will survive this. She seemed like such a nice lady. She kept calling her son 'my baby'...All that motherly love, and still this boy turns into a plain gangster." She shakes her head in disapproval.

"Love is not always enough to save someone," I reply while staring at the patient. "If a person were an empty shell, then maybe you could fill him or her with affection, but each one of us has dark corners in our souls that no light of love can illuminate." I hear Ms. MJ shuffle away, mumbling something under her breath. She has to continue the duties of her shift, and I go to prepare for the sign out. When I am finished signing out my patients to the next resident, I head straight for the garage to meet Leo, as we agreed. Leo opens the passenger door for me and then takes his seat behind the wheel. The turn of the key makes the engine rumble, but the sound is not that of a powerful beast, but rather that of a coughing, sick, mechanical monster.

"C'mon, c'mon—don't do this now," Leo begs. He turns the key again, but this time more gently. The car purrs loudly. "Good girl! See, I told you she is moody." I smile at Leo's relationship with his car, happy we are able to drive off and leave the hospital behind.

"It is so strange to have the awareness that I am alive at this moment when I just witnessed another person lose his life." I voice my thoughts to Leo, remembering the death of the boy at the end of the day.

"Don't feel bad for that patient...he wasn't a good person. Last year, he came in after shooting a rival gang member and one of the bullets from the shoot-out pierced the wall of a nearby building, killing a child. The child died in his bed; this guy unfortunately got another chance, and look—he ended up wasting it again. He shouldn't have made it the first time around." I stare at Leo who looks so calm and relaxed behind the wheel of his car. The thought of the bad guy doesn't disturb his handsome face.

"I feel badly for his mother. I caught a glimpse of her when she got to the ER. Do you think she realized that her son was a bad guy? Do you think she loved him less?" I seek answers to questions that puzzle my consciousness.

"I really don't know," he shrugs his shoulders, looking ahead at the road, "but I think when you love someone, you will never see them as bad. They are flawed, for sure, but then it is easier to find excuses for the flaws. I had to tell her that her son had passed away. She looked relieved; she didn't cry at all. All she said was that he is in a better place now and thanked me for trying to bring him back."

"Hmm…" I let the silence overtake the space between us as I look out the car window. The Camaro sounds like a living beast, propelling us forward with the loud heartbeat of its engine.

"You will meet a lot of patients in your career. Some you will just remember by their diagnosis; some by just the number of the room that they were in. There are some that will make you regret you ever went into medicine, and then there are some that will remind you that you saved them, really saved them, and that they appreciate this enormous gift of life and they appreciate you. Those are the patients that I work for: they are the ones that make it all worthwhile and make it possible to survive all the other bullshit. You just have to find something like that—something that will make you work another hour, another day." He gives a gentle squeeze of my knee. I take his hand into mine and give a kiss to the rough skin of his palm.

"Do you have any flaws?" I take an innocent jab at him. His eyebrows furrow and I see his jaw tighten.

"I have a past, Mila, that I am not very proud of. I don't want to scare you off with the details, but when I finished residency, the power of having the skills to bring someone back, acting at a moment's notice…that adrenalin really got to me. I was constantly looking for the next high; work wasn't always enough. So, to supplement, I turned to women and unfortunately, it was too easy to find willing women at work. I was just looking for instant gratification, but it didn't always hold true for the women, so I hurt many of them. That is why I want to keep our relationship a secret for now—I don't want you to be targeted because of my poor choices in the past." He takes his eyes off the road to quickly glance at my reaction. I wonder if my silence is making him nervous, but I need to collect my thoughts before I speak. Leo's brows furrow even more than before; he runs his hand through his hair. I don't want him to regret his honesty.

"How do I know that this is all in the past? How do I know that I am not just another woman in the crowd of many before me?" We come off Brooklyn's Queens expressway at Ridge Blvd. and Leo parks his car at Owl's Head Park, just a block from my apartment. The lush greens serve as a getaway from the concrete and asphalt of surrounding streets. Narrow paths twist and turn as they go up a steep hill where a picturesque view of the bay offers tranquility. The evening is warm and not windy: the waters must be calm and we will certainly see the New York skyline from across the bay. Leo exits the car in silence and comes around to open the door for me. His out-stretched arm helps me up from the low seats of his beloved Camaro, and pulls me directly towards him. Leo's hand lifts my chin up so that I cannot avoid looking into his eyes.

"Don't you see you how much I want you? You can't imagine how much I would love for us to take it further… but I am following your lead. Your happiness is most important to me; I will do anything to gain your trust, OK?" For now, I am satisfied by his answer and I feel myself staring at his full lips, drawn towards them by forceful gravity. Our lips collide in a passionate, hungry kiss, resulting in a pleasantly ticklish eruption in the pit of my belly. Leo tears himself away from the kiss, with a fire still visible in his honey-colored eyes.

"Let's go for that walk." He takes me by the hand and we follow the path along the edge of the park leading to the Belt Parkway underpass. We walk underneath the busy roadway, and emerge on the boardwalk with a long pier stretching out before us. The waters are mirror calm, and the salty smell of the ocean fills our lungs. We stroll in enjoyable silence towards the pier, hand in hand, with a view of the Manhattan skyscrapers to the right. They are like ever-reaching pillars, trying to support the invisible roof above them; on the left, there is Verrazano Bridge, seemingly floating above the water.

"I love it here." I admit, taking a deep breath in of the salty air. "I feel like everything is within my reach… I just have to make the effort."

"What would you like to reach?" Leo asks when we get to the end of the pier, the side overlooking Manhattan. He lets go of my hand, moves close behind me, and hugs me tight. His head rests on my shoulder so that I feel the roughness of his unshaven face with my cheek, and we both stare out into the coldness of the city.

"I guess mostly peace and happiness—just like everyone else."

"I would argue with you on that. You are far from being like everyone else, and everyone else doesn't just want peace and happiness," he chuckles softly.

"Why are you such a pessimist?"

"Hmmm...I don't think I am. I do not look at things or people as hopeless. I think I am more of a realist," he replies in his low voice.

"So, what is it that you want in life?"

"I want to be happy. I want a family, a successful career, and good health, just like everyone else." He chuckles again and I feel the warmth of his breath on my neck and then a soft kiss that makes me snuggle into the embrace even more. We stand like that for a few minutes and then decide to stroll down the boardwalk towards Verrazano Bridge. Our pace is slow; our hands are still clasped, swinging widely as we walk. Everyone we pass by seems to be enjoying a beautiful evening. Some are running, cycling, or rollerblading; a few families are out teaching their kids how to ride a bicycle. Teenage couples occupy the benches, hunched over, whispering and giggling. A crowd of young singles are chatting and smoking to the beat of a boom box the size of which I have seen in eighties videos.

An elderly couple, probably in their seventies, approaches the crowd and shake their heads in disapproval. We pass each other, couples both young and old; we smile, acknowledging each other's presence and different stages of relationship. I wonder if they wish to be young again and if Leo and I will walk hand in hand at their age. The old woman wraps her arm around her husband and puts her head on his shoulder; he kisses her hair softly and pats her hand. I smile and look away, feeling like I am intruding on their intimate moment. Leo grabs my hand and kisses it softly, submerging me into an intimate moment of our own, but the moment is gone once we hear a loud gasp. We turn around in the direction of the gasp to find the elderly man nearly on the ground, and his wife standing frozen over him, her arm still hanging onto his. With only a few steps separating us, both Leo and I reach them quickly. Leo introduces himself and me to the elderly woman, who still stands in shock.

"Ma'am! You have to call 911!" Leo yells to the woman.

"Misha, Misha—up, up." She starts to wail, ignoring Leo's instructions. I get the breathing mask out of my bag, thankful that I decided to carry it with me ever since my first-aid training. After determining that the elderly man is not breathing, I blow two breaths through the mask into his mouth. A crowd starts to gather. Leo gets one of the nearby teenagers to dial 911. I hear the wife still screaming for her husband, now in Russian. I can understand that she is telling him to get up, but having little practice in conversational Russian, I only manage to say that everything will be all right as Leo performs chest compressions. She nods her head to my empty reassurance. Leo finishes the first round of compressions and I blow five more breaths into the elderly's man body, then check his pulse. I shake my head to Leo that none is found, and he starts the compressions again.

The crowd of onlookers close in on us and I have to tell them to step back because we need air. I think they listen. I stop hearing the woman's crying, and I don't see the faces in the crowd. In that moment, I can feel my own heartbeat and I count compressions before the next set of breaths that I have to blow into the unmoving body. The woman collapses to her knees near her man and for a brief moment, she manages to collect herself. She asks me in Russian: Why is he—her husband—lying down? My mind races trying to look through piles of rarely used language for the correct words, but all I manage to produce is that the he is sick, and help is coming. I'm not making enough sense to her, or maybe my accent is too thick, but she looks at me, puzzled, and like the siren of the approaching ambulance, she starts to cry again.

The ambulance reaches us in under three minutes, but it feels like at least half an hour has passed. The defibrillator establishes asystole, and the elderly man is taken to the hospital. I don't know how long I have been standing still, staring into the distance long after the ambulance has disappeared, but I feel a soft squeeze of my shoulder. A kiss on the head from Leo unfreezes me, and I realize that the sun has already set, and the crowd that had surrounded us has dispersed.

"Come...I will take you home," Leo whispers softly and takes my hand into his.

"Work sure follows you around," I tell him.

"Are you sure it follows me? How are you doing?" he questions.

"I am fine." I breathe out.

"Here—you left this on the ground." Leo passes me the breathing mask.

"You know, when I initially finished first-aid training, I wanted so badly to use this on someone. Today I feel so guilty for my wishful thinking." I stare at the plastic breathing mask that I had just used to deliver air into the elderly man's lungs.

"Don't…You might have saved his life." We walk the rest of the way to my apartment building in silence. Tonight, Leo walks me right up to the door. I know he will not try to come inside, but today I ask him in. To my disappointment, he shakes his head no.

"Can't we just get some sleep together? I swear I am too tired for anything else." I just want to feel his embrace as I drift off to sleep; I know it will make me feel secure.

"Ah, you won't be able to sway me, woman. Go and get some rest." He plants a long, soft goodnight kiss on the inside of my wrist and then offers a quick peck on my lips before turning away and taking the stairs. I smile at his sweet commitment to taking our relationship slowly, and shuffle my tired mind and body into the apartment.

"Hey girl! We are watching a movie. Come join us," Michelle yells out cheerfully from the living room, probably all cozied up to her boyfriend.

"No thanks. I am going to take a shower and collapse if you don't mind." I don't want to feel like a third wheel.

"I put your mail under your bedroom door."

"Thanks. Good night, guys!" I take a long shower, trying to wash away the hospital smell. I close my eyes and let the warm water wash over my face. I come out clean but exhausted, and schlep my way to the bedroom. I step over the pile of mail that usually contains credit card offers, and car insurance advertisements for the car that I don't have. I climb into bed and fall into an uneasy and restless sleep, filled with dreams of me running from room to room, trying to save patients, but all my efforts prove futile.

CHAPTER 12

"Are you ready, Dr. Roth?" Dr. Kim asks me after the rounds. I try to respond confidently in the affirmative, hoping to hide my exhaustion. *One more shift after this one and I have a day off*, I say to myself, imagining myself sleeping in.

It is hard to tell how old Dr. Kim is...His possible age range is wide—somewhere between forty-five and sixty. His skin is smooth, lacking any age-telling wrinkles, and his hair is dusted with few greys. Dr. Kim is known as the most hard-working attending in this emergency department: while most physicians do twelve to sixteen shifts a month, he, on average, does twenty. Dr. Kim is always calm and collected: no one ever hears him raise his voice at a resident, another attending, or a patient. He seems to have endless patience in teaching everyone who is willing to learn. He listens to patients' nervous explanations, not rushing through the procedures and, most importantly, being interested in the well-being of each person he encounters. He is rumored to be divorced, due to his demanding work schedule. I overheard him say once, "Medicine is my first and only love." I decide that no woman has a chance to win in that competition.

"Walk with me; I want to see this patient together and see what you think. This is a twenty-one-year-old male who felt sharp chest pain, and had difficulty breathing. What would be your differential diagnosis?"

"Spontaneous pneumothorax," I answer confidently.

"Excellent! What side would the trachea be deviated to on his X-ray?" Dr. Kim quizzes me as we continue walking.

"The side of the collapsed lung, unless it is tension pneumothorax. Then, the trachea will be deviated to the opposite side."

"Excellent. And what would be the procedure of choice for this patient?"

"Chest tube, of course," I continue answering promptly.

"Have you ever done one, Dr. Roth?"

"No."

"Excellent! Today is your lucky day. Go on in. Let's meet your patient." Dr. Kim nudges me as I pause before the curtain separating us from the patient.

When we go in, I introduce myself. Dr. Kim explains the procedure while I prepare the supplies. The young man is thin and tall; his long, slim fingers clasp the blanket nervously. I ask him if he has Marfan syndrome—a genetic condition that predisposes to spontaneous pneumothorax. He nods his head yes to my inquiry.

Dr. Kim voices another, "Excellent," and motions for me to begin. I prep the skin over the side of the collapsed lung with iodine, then I inject an anesthetic that makes the patient squirm. I offer my apologies for causing the discomfort but proceed nevertheless, taking the scalpel and making a cut in the soft space between the ribs, right where the anesthetic was injected. The patient lays still, indicating that he is not feeling any pain.

"OK, Dr. Roth—now insert your index finger and feel the intercostal space; you have to separate the muscle to create the space for the chest tube."

I proceed slowly and do exactly as Dr. Kim tells me. When my gloved finger enters the space created by my scalpel, I feel the instant heat of the patient's body. The muscle fibers are soft but tightly interwoven, holding the ribs together. I dig in and feel the squeeze of the ribs on my fingers. When I hear a soft escape of air, I know I've entered the thoracic cavity. Dr. Kim helps me insert the tube and takes over to suture it into place. I finish by placing a dressing over the necessary wound that I have created, and explain to the patient that he will be transferred to the medical floor in a little while.

"Excellent work, Dr. Roth," he says after the procedure. "You stayed cool under pressure. If you love doing procedures, I will be happy to teach them. Write up your procedure note while I check on what is next."

I find an empty spot by the nurses station and start charting the procedure that I just performed. There are always people by the station: students, physicians, nurses and PAs...Everyone is busy doing their work. I have learned not to be distracted by constant noise and commotion, but this time I feel a gaze upon me. I look up to find the person who is staring at me.

"Dr. Bryce, hi! Can I help you with something?"

"Hi Dr. Roth! I didn't appreciate the little stunt that you pulled yesterday. I already work hard, and I had to work even harder because you wanted to play 'good doctor'," she whispers with menace.

"Dr. Bryce, first of all: back off—you are in my space. Second of all, I was doing my job…making sure I treat the patient, and not Dr. Kramer's ego. Third, if Dr. Kramer has a problem with me, I can handle it. I suggest that if you have a problem with him, you do the same. I am not your enemy here: I am a resident, just like you." Dr. Bryce steps back, probably surprised by my not mincing words. She looks down at me and purses her lips.

"Fine—be the good doctor, but believe me, I will be watching you. Make sure you don't screw up."

"And I will watch that you don't screw up," I throw right back at her.

She flings her hair back; I am sure she is dissatisfied with her attempt to scare me and she walks off into the depths of the department. I learned a long time ago not to be easily intimidated. When I was about to cry, and refuse to go outside or to school because I was upset over some misfortune that had befallen me, my grandmother used to say, "Not one step back! Behind is Moscow." This was a saying popular in Russia during World War II, calling on people to fight back until their last breath and not retreat, otherwise the capital of the Soviet Union would be taken by the Nazis. Grandmother would wipe my tears, look straight into my eyes and motion for me to take a deep breath so that my tears wouldn't turn into sobbing, and a full-on meltdown.

"Mila, you are a strong girl. Always believe in yourself and what you know. There will be people who cast doubt about who you are as a person, and how knowledgeable you are. You have to study hard so that you never falter. If you do falter, then you have to study more." The playground has since gotten bigger, other kids grew up, and their threats got scarier, but my persistence in holding my ground has never faltered. I know that I had made the right call with Mr. Saymore…Dr. Bryce can't frighten me with her threats.

When my note is done, I see the other patients that have come up on the schedule, and write my notes for them as well. Dr. Kim keeps me busy, letting me perform several more procedures. He walks me through the insertion of the central line for a patient that was found unconscious on his job; I suture a lip laceration, meticulously aligning the lip border, so the patient has the best cosmetic outcome. I also evaluate a patient with a ruptured appendix, and impress Dr. Kim when I recognize a patient's rash as shingles.

"Dr. Roth, you are doing great today," Dr. Kim praises me.

"Thank you, Dr. Kim. I love what I do. Thank you for teaching me today."

"My pleasure. Don't forget this feeling of loving what you do. There will be days and weeks when you will feel the complete opposite: defeated, and regretful, but remember why you went into medicine…You are making a difference—remember that!" I nod, thankful for his pep talk.

My shift ends and I am happy to go home. I didn't have time to eat, and had to make a run to the bathroom by the end of the rounds to avoid a rupture of my bladder.

While walking towards the exit, I bump into Max Kogan's mother. She is dressed in a velour jumpsuit of deep purple with perfectly matching lipstick. Her hair is as stiff as ever, untouched by the outside humidity. She peeks at me from under her sunglasses before saying hello.

"Hi Mila!"

"What are you doing here? I thought you were going to arrange for Max's transfer to another hospital," I say, hiding my unhappiness that her son is still nearby.

"Oh no, no, no. Our cardiologist suggested that Max stays here. He was concerned that Max was not stable enough for the transfer. Look at the things I have to bring in," she points to her many shopping bags. "The food here is just terrible." She shakes her head disapprovingly. "I brought some organic oranges and apples, and made some home-cooked meatballs and mashed potatoes, and of course, my famous cabbage pie—everything just like Max loves."

"I don't know if he is allowed to eat all of that: you better ask his doctor," I suggest to this woman who probably never takes anyone's advice.

"Of course he can eat that! There is nothing better than my cooking!" She takes offense and I see where Max gets his obnoxious confidence.

"If you would like, I can give you the recipes; then you would just make a perfect wife for my Max." She manages to judge, and put me down, all in one sentence.

"Mrs. Kogan, I am sorry to disappoint you, but Max and I are not going to happen...*ever*!" I stress the last word, hoping that Max's mother will get it through her stiff hair and her thick layer of pretentiousness that any effort to bring her son and I together is pointless. Mrs. Kogan purses her lips, and looks me up and down as if processing my words as something unimaginable.

"Any girl would be lucky to marry my son...It is your loss, Mila. Well, anyway, I have to go before the food gets cold. Goodbye!" she snaps as she collects her bags and walks away, holding her head way too high.

"Bye." I shake my head at this woman who thinks that she is better than everyone else and hope that Max gets discharged soon, so I don't have to see either of them again.

I finally make it outside; the sunshine feels warm on my skin. I put my face to the sky and close my eyes for a brief moment. The loud roaring of an engine attracts my attention. I look in the direction of the sound and find a biker dressed in a black leather jacket with his head and face covered by the same color helmet. He waves, and I look around to see if the wave is meant for me or somebody else. He waves again, but I decide against approaching the stranger and start walking towards the train station. I am able to make just a few steps before I hear a familiar voice calling my name. I look back and now that the helmet is off, I see that the biker is Leo.

"Hey! I didn't recognize you!" I walk up to him happily.

"Sorry—should have taken off my helmet. It's just a pain to take it on and off..." He smiles apologetically and draws me in for a kiss. "Hi! How was your day? Are you tired? Hungry?"

"Famished and exhausted," I sigh.

"Come; I will feed you." He hands me a spare helmet.

"Where are you taking me?" I inquire.

"My place. I want you to meet someone, and I am making you dinner," he replies nonchalantly, not giving me any opportunity to object, not that I really want to.

"You cook?" I tease him.

"Sometimes…but only for people who are special to me." He takes the helmet out of my hands and puts it on my head, tightening the buckle gently as I pause unexpectedly from his admission.

"Who am I meeting?"

"You will find out soon enough. Climb on, and hold tight." I follow his instructions willingly, curious about the surprise meeting.

CHAPTER 13

"You have a dog! Oh my goodness! What is his name?" I pet a friendly beast of unknown breed when we finally make it to Leo's apartment. The dog comes up to just above my knee; his short coat is of caramel color, and a white stripe runs from the tip of his nose to between his ears. The color of his eyes is a striking, icy blue. "What kind of a dog is he? He is beautiful!"

"He is a mix of lab and husky," Leo replies as the dog licks my face before running circles around me, and then flopping belly up, inviting me to give him a scratch.

"His name is Boss," Leo says, leaning against the wall, observing his four-legged friend welcoming me. "He's taken a liking to you and that dog is a terrible grouch who generally doesn't like anyone."

"This guy? A grouch? No! You are a good boy! You are such a good boy!" I keep petting Boss, who now is trying to jump on me and happily wagging his tail.

"All right, all right, Boss! Enough! Don't embarrass me in front of this girl. Behave! Sit!" On command, the dog sits still, waiting for more directions.

"Is this who you wanted me to meet?" I ask Leo.

"Uh-huh," Leo grunts. "I want you to meet everyone who is important to me, and this guy's approval is the most valuable and unbiased." He smiles and rubs Boss between the ears.

"So, does he approve of me?" I stare at the dog who keeps looking back and forth at both of us as if understanding that the conversation involves him, and that he is a decisive factor in our relationship.

Leo laughs, throwing his head back. "I think he loves you." Boss barks, confirming Leo's statement, and then licks my hand that has been scratching his snout.

"Why did you name him Boss? It is such a funny name for a dog."

"My whole schedule has revolved around him since he was a pup. My decisions also always involve him, so it just felt appropriate to call him that." Leo satisfies my curiosity and we proceed into the living room with Boss walking by my side. Leo gives me a quick tour of his unremarkable apartment that has only the bare necessities. He then invites me to sit down at the kitchen island as he starts preparing dinner.

"Is that your grandfather?" I point at the elderly man in the picture with Leo. Leo is dressed in cap and gown and is holding his medical school diploma. In the picture, a wide smile of satisfaction beams across Leo's face. His grandfather is just as happy, throwing him a proud 'thumbs up'. Both have similarly strong chins, square jaws, even the shape of their lips gives away that they are related.

"Yes, it is," Leo affirms. He pauses for a moment and smiles, looking at the picture that sits in the center of the island.

"What happened to him?" I ask this because his grandfather is in a wheelchair. His left eye is covered with a patch—a noticeable facial concavity of the eye area means that severe trauma to the head has been suffered— and both of his legs are amputated below the knee.

This time, Leo stops his cooking altogether and comes over to me, so that we are both facing the picture. His arm wraps around my waist and he brings me closer to him as he begins to tell the story of his grandfather's injuries. I place my head against Leo's chest.

"This man was truly incredible," Leo begins, taking the picture into his hands. "It is hard to imagine the hardships that he overcame and still stayed so positive. He was an inspiration as to how to live a life of joy. He used to tell me: "Live each day, so the morning of the next, you don't regret the hours that passed." He served in World War II. My grandmother was the one who found him…I guess his battalion was attacked and there were no other survivors. He was hit with shrapnel and lost his eye. Because of hours spent lying in the freezing cold, he got frostbite and lost both of his legs.

"My grandmother's father was a local butcher slash doctor, if you can imagine, and he was able to take care of my grandfather, and hide him from the Nazis. They found no documents on him and because of his head trauma, he suffered with retrograde amnesia. Grandfather would tell me about getting flashbacks of places and faces, but nothing specific enough to give him names or addresses. The only place he saw clearly in his mind was Saint Petersburg, it was called

Leningrad before. He visited it many times; he loved that city. When he died, I took his ashes there and spread them over Neva."

"What was his name?"

"His new name was Genadiy, but no one really knew his real name. He took the last name of my grandmother. After the war, they were able to emigrate to Israel and then the States. Here, he became a mechanic; he was always tinkering with things. His garage was a fascinating place, full of mechanical things. I guess that's why I love fixing cars…it was something I picked up from him." Leo puts down the picture and I feel his chest rise and fall in a sigh.

"Come; the food is almost ready."

"My grandmother lived in Saint Petersburg during World War Two. I am going over her letters to her fiancé and they are just heartbreaking. It was a terrible time." I move from the island to the dinner table.

"Yes, it was." He pulls out a chair for me at the table and places a paper towel over my knees.

"Sorry, I'm not fancy enough to have cloth napkins. I usually eat by myself and don't require any."

"It's all right—I am not fancy enough to expect one," I joke.

The food is simple, but delicious: baked salmon, mushroom risotto, and a garden salad. We wash it down with an apple-flavored cider and I feel completely stuffed.

"I could just fall asleep right now," I mumble.

"I would love for you to stay over," Leo admits, giving my hand a light squeeze, "but you still have to meet my parents and I have one more day at the hospital.

I promised I would behave until then." He smiles and his eyes twinkle with mischief. "Let's go; I will take you home." After I pet Boss and say goodbye to my new furry friend, Leo takes my hand and we walk outside. The sun has already set, but the last far-reaching rays keep the evening bathed in light. The street is noisy with passing cars; there is the chatter of people from the benches in the courtyard, and the screams of little kids from the nearby park.

Leo hands me a helmet and is about to straddle his bike, but he pauses when he sees a piece of folded paper attached to the small windshield of his vehicle.

"What is it?" I ask as his jaw tightens. He purses his lips and furrows his brows.

Leo reads the handwritten note and hesitates for a moment, but then he passes it to me to read.

Leo,

I am not able to speak to you face to face, but I need you to hear me out. Remember, I love you! I care for you deeply and I want to warn you about Dr. Roth. She is lying to you and wants to use you for her own advancement. Be careful around her and don't trust her. I am the only one for you. We will be together soon. Yours, loving guardian angel!

"Who the hell is this person?! And how does she even know who I am?! She says she loves you? What are you not telling me, Leo?" I angrily clump up the piece of paper and shove it into his hand.

"I have my suspicions," Leo says calmly while staring at his fist that closes tightly over the note.

His jaw clenches, he presses his hand over his eyes, taking deep breaths.

"I cannot believe how calm you are about this!"

"Mila, please do not be angry. People who do this kind of stuff—they yearn for this reaction; they want you to panic and be irrational. I think I know who it might be. Please let me take care of it."

"Are you going to go to the police?!"

"The police are already involved."

"What do you mean?! This is not the first letter?!" I yell at Leo.

"No, it is not. I wanted to tell you about this at a better time. I didn't want to scare you off with this complication, but I guess at this point I better come clean." He shifts his weight from one leg to the other.

"Let's go back to the apartment and speak there," Leo suggests, looking around, probably uncomfortable from the looks the passersby are giving us.

"Tell me everything! You promised to be honest with me!" I demand angrily as I shove the helmet back to him. I want to hear his answers now, before he has time to think over his words. The last rays of the sun have disappeared and the street lights take over.

He hangs the spare helmet on the handle of the bike and grabs me by the shoulders. "Mila, look into my eyes and promise me you will not panic and decide that this is all too much for you, OK?" His warm gaze holds mine hostage and doesn't let go until I comply.

"Tell me everything," I demand of him, without making any other promises.

"The woman who wrote this letter…her name is Laura. She was a patient of mine once, and has developed an infatuation with me. I have a restraining order against her, but she has been ignoring it. I will file another police report, especially since she has mentioned you in this note. I am really sorry that you got dragged into this." His head hangs low, waiting for my judgment; his hand reaches for mine, but I pull away.

"Why didn't you tell me this before?"

"A stalker is not something you reveal to a girl that you really like. I was afraid you might run for the hills; I didn't want to scare you off."

"You should have let me know, and then let me decide how to behave." I feel uneasy about this woman. How is it that she feels so much for him? Did he lead her on? Did he act inappropriately, or is she plain crazy? I have to think it all over—there are too many questions and not enough answers.

"I'm sorry. I understand how upset you must be with me, but believe me, I didn't want to hide it from you, I just wanted to wait for a good time to tell you all of it." He raises his hand palm up, and this time I give him my hand. He wraps his fingers around mine and brings my hands to his lips. He places a soft kiss and his eyes look directly into mine; I know he is being honest with me.

"It would have been better if you told me before… before you got this note," I admonish him. "Please take me home," I ask. He quietly obliges.

Leo must understand that I need time to digest all this new information and decide how to react to it.

We get on the bike and race through the streets and the parkway. The sound of the bike piercing the air floods my senses, suppressing the noise of my thoughts. I wrap my hands tightly around Leo's body, feeling the hardness of his muscles. I wonder about the woman who feels that Leo should love her.

The rumbling of the engine steadies my breathing and thoughts. I begin to understand why Leo waited to tell me about his stalker. Not everyone would be willing to deal with the added complication of a possibly dangerous stalker in a new relationship. I question if this complication scares me. I decide to sleep on it and think more about it tomorrow: tomorrow it will make more sense. We pull up to the apartment building. The street is deserted, and the high humidity is setting in as night falls on the city. Leo stays still on the bike, waiting for me to get off and take off my helmet.

"I need to see you." I ask him to take off his helmet, but before he does, I stare at the reflection in the visor for a few moments: his usually sunny eyes look dark and gloomy. Helmet off, he gives me a quick glance and looks away. I put my palm onto his cheek and turn his head to force him to look straight into my eyes.

"Laura doesn't scare me...I am more scared of the unknown. Believe me, I can handle a lot, but I will not tolerate lies. I don't want her to be a shadow over us. I wish I was made aware of her existence earlier."

Leo puts his hand on top of mine and kisses the inside of my wrist. "I didn't mean to lie to you, Mila. I hate that Laura has tarnished our relationship. I have never felt so strongly about anyone else; I wouldn't want to hurt you. Please believe me."

"I believe you." I reach out to him and run my fingers through his hair. He leans his head into my palm.

"Go rest...You've had a long day. I am sorry it ended this way."

"Please don't apologize. You cannot control everything and certainly not people with mental problems."

I put my other hand on Leo's face and press my forehead against his. "Laura's nadir doesn't cast a shadow on us," I whisper, staring right into the warmth of his gaze.

Leo leans in and kisses my lips softly. My lips part and I graze his lips with my tongue. His caution disappears, and he greets my tongue with his, bringing me close to his body with a firm grip around my waist.

He tears himself from my lips, breathless. "Go rest! I will call you tomorrow." His eyes are glowing warm again. I nod and plant a quick peck on his nose. When I close the door behind me, I hear the engine of his bike, taking Leo away from my place.

CHAPTER 14

L eo drove home, thinking of Mila and how she made him feel. She had entered his life like a brush fire, burning all the uncertainty and doubt into ash. He was drawn to her strength—she made him believe in goodness once again. Mila's blue eyes peered deep into his soul: he wanted her to know all of him. He wanted to make her happy, and to keep her safe. He was concerned about Laura becoming unhinged and now threatening Mila. He could no longer feel bad for Laura because it would be at the cost of Mila's safety. He got home fast. He ran up the stairs instead of taking the slow elevator and reached his apartment on autopilot, not paying much attention to his surroundings. In the narrow hallway, reaching into his pocket for the keys, he looked up and saw Laura, pacing, just outside his apartment.

She had shaved the rest of her hair and now looked like a prematurely aged, angry child. Her bloodshot eyes darted back and forth, her left hand wouldn't stay still; she either wiped her nose obsessively with the back of her hand, or scratched her naked scalp. When her hand couldn't find her hair, she bit her nails. She was a woman on a sinister mission. Leo was relieved that Mila had already left; he knew that this time, the encounter with Laura would not end well.

"What are you doing here, Laura? You know you cannot come around! I will have to call the cops this time," Leo said angrily, through his teeth. It was good that he had finally filed a restraining order against her and installed the camera above his door. He had been afraid that one day, she would come too close.

"Don't bother—I will call them myself. Why can't you love me? What does she have that I don't?" Laura fired off disconnected questions, anger escalating her voice to a high pitch.

"Don't bring Mila into this and don't you dare contact her. Call the cops…I will happily speak to them. I hope prison time will give you some perspective." Leo lost his usual cool when Laura mentioned Mila. He didn't want anything to happen to her: she had become too precious in his life.

"I am not going to prison, you are! I am tired of you pushing me aside. This time, you will not be able to just dismiss me. I will be part of your life, dead or alive." Her hand dove into a pocket of her baggy pants and she revealed a large kitchen knife. Her right hand held the phone. "Please…please help me—he is trying to kill me! Come fast to 2035 Court Street. Please hurry!" Laura screamed into the phone, her voice trembling in pretentious fear.

"What the fuck are you saying, Laura? You are completely insane! Put the knife down. I am not trying to hurt you!" Leo didn't anticipate this turn of events at all. Laura had become completely desperate in her obsession with him. He understood that she didn't value her life anymore, that she felt scorned by Leo not returning her affection. He realized he had to act with extreme caution and try to change her train of thought.

"Then kiss me, and I will put the knife down," she whispered. Her eyes shone with menace, her nostrils flared, and she nervously licked her lips. Leo made a careful step forward, he watched the arm holding the knife relax, he lunged, but Laura was nimble and fast and drove a knee into his crotch. The pain took his breath away and sent him to the floor.

"You wouldn't even kiss me to save me? What kind of a person are you? You do not deserve to have me! I will haunt you for the rest of your life!" The sound of police sirens announced their approach. The bright lights reflected on the walls inside Leo's apartment building and on the blade in Laura's hand, it flew high and sunk into the soft flesh of her belly. Finally, she was still...Her eyes met his and for the first time, he saw the clarity of her thinking, as if a veil of obsession was lifted off by the pain she'd inflicted on herself. She stood there in front of him, bent over, her eyes transfixed on something. A few seconds later she fell to her knees. Leo stepped up to catch her from falling on the cold, hard floor. Her eyes flooded with tears, she grabbed onto his arms. "I am sorry!" she mouthed and her body went limp.

"Sir, step away from her. Slowly!" The order was barked behind Leo's back.

"I am a doctor. She needs help!"

"I think you've helped enough!" Leo's hands were forced behind his back and put into cuffs. His phone slipped out of his pocket, the fragile glass of the screen was stepped on and broken by the boots of the law.

"I didn't hurt her! She did it to herself!"

"Whatever you say, man, but anything you say can and will be used against you in a court of law." Leo was read his Miranda rights, brought downstairs, and shoved into the squad car. The street was flooded with more emergency vehicles, all rushing to save Laura.

CHAPTER 15

I wake up with a headache and I am still tired. I lay in my bed without stirring, staring at the ray of sunlight moving slowly across my ceiling. My cell phone alarm begins to sound, the rush of waves announcing that it is 6:45 a.m. and I should consider getting up.

"OK, OK, I heard you! I should have turned you off." I bicker with the piece of modern technology.

I shut the alarm off and refuse to get out of bed just yet. Thoughts of the previous evening start to roll in their tidal waves, flooding my brain. I get even more lost and exhausted trying to swim against the current of common sense, which is telling me that I am stupid for getting involved with Leo. But my heart keeps propelling me, pushing me ahead with the promise of a safe haven—a happy ending. There is something that makes me trust Leo…I believe his feelings, but the knowledge or rather lack of it about that other woman makes me uneasy.

I decide to talk to Michelle, hoping that by voicing my feelings about Leo to her I will somehow gain some much-needed clarity.

When my phone shows that it is 7:00 a.m., I tippy-toe to Michelle's bedroom, trying to preserve the morning silence. I climb up right next to my sleeping friend.

"Good morning, you sleepy head!"

"What time is it?!" Michelle growls at my intrusion and pulls the covers over her head, shielding herself from my morning assault on her day off sleeping-in habit.

"I don't know," I lie to my friend, "but I don't think it is that early."

"I know you are lying. You better have a good reason for waking me up." Her voice is muffled and sleepy.

"You know, my grandmother used to say that early risers get God's blessings, or something like that."

"Mila, I am going to try and stay half asleep hoping that you will leave me be and I can fall back into blissful sleep and stay asleep until it is late—very, very late. And please don't bring God into this. I did four twelve-hour shifts in a row; I deserve to be blessed with sleep."

"Leo received a fan letter yesterday…" I pause to see if this bit of information perks my friend up and out of her sleep, but she only mumbles something indistinguishable under her breath and continues to lay curled up with her back towards me.

"The woman professed her undying love for Leo, and warned him against me…Can you imagine!?" I say this with as much exasperation as possible, but even that doesn't wake my friend up from her slumber. She acknowledges my talking by emitting a loud snore.

"Hey—did you hear what I just said?" I give her a firm nudge that startles her and she sits up and finally faces me.

"Grrr…You owe me for this morning wake-up call. How do you know it is a woman?"

"Huh? What are you talking about?"

"How do you know that it was a woman who wrote to him?"

"You are so stupid!" I giggle at my friend's humorous proposition. "But seriously?"

"Honestly, I am not surprised. I keep telling you that he has some baggage and that baggage has just arrived. I just don't understand how someone like you got involved with someone like him."

"Someone like me?" I look puzzled, waiting for her definition of me.

"You know…You are so proper. Your life is so organized, or was, until you met this guy. You seem like a person who has everything figured out and you generally don't take any bullshit from men; you run away at the first sign of a red flag. But for some reason, you are just stuck on this guy."

"I know—I cannot explain it or rationalize it, but for some reason, I trust him."

"Why?" Michelle presses me for an explanation.

"I don't know why!" I snap. "I believe him because so far, he has been sincere with me. I have only known him for less than a week: I can't expect him to just spill everything from his past life, just like that."

"Mila, I hope your gut doesn't betray you. I have to know all the dirt upfront. I have to know about all the freaky ex-girlfriends and baby mamas before I even consider going on a first date. I lay out the rules of being with me on the first date. My man needs to know all the rewards and consequences of stepping left or right when he is with me."

"Geez Michelle, you are tough...Poor Rob."

"No, no, no—he is happy. There are no games that he has to play with me. I am straightforward, and he likes that," she says with unshakable confidence. "It is not that I don't believe in love—I do. But I want it to be on my terms. I want to control my destiny."

"But you do realize there is another person involved, don't you?" I question Michelle, but I already know that she will always protect her feelings first, before she becomes vulnerable, even with a man she truly loves.

"Well, he would just have to accept me and my rules."

"You can't think that it is fair, can you?" I challenge her.

"I don't. But life is not fair." Michelle shrugs her shoulders. "I know, I sound like I don't care about him. I love him, really. But I am not willing to lose myself just so that we can have a relationship. I don't need him to be my other half. I am a whole person, and he is a whole person. We are not less without each other."

"But you are more together," I say, smiling to my friend.

"Mila, you are such a romantic. How is it that you are still single?" she stings me with the question.

"You know why: you yourself call me a book-worm." I remind her of the reason for my prolonged single status.

"Well, look at you now…You've gotten yourself into some dating mess, and since you woke me up to tell me about it, you now have to go to IKEA with me."

"OK, Ms. Bossy. What are we buying?"

"I have to buy pillows and curtains and some chuchkies for Rob's place. This guy has no colors other than black, grey, or white. I told him that if he wants me to move in, he has to let me decorate." Michelle gets out of bed, dancing to her own tune.

"You are moving out?"

"No…He has to put a ring on my finger first. I am just making his place more suitable for me."

"Does he know that?"

"Yes, of course he does. He knows the size of my finger, the shape of the stone, and the setting that I want if he wants to marry me."

"You are kidding, right?"

"No. I am telling you—guys are animals and as animals they need rules to obey; they need structure, and they need an owner: an 'alpha' if you want to make it sound better. In my relationships, I am the alpha. I set the rules and structure. All dogs are happy when they have a good owner."

"Don't you think you are oversimplifying it just a tiny bit?"

Michelle looks somewhere into the distance, maybe giving my thought a split second of her consideration, and with a confident shrug of her shoulders and shake of her head she tells me, "No." She continues to dress in silence while I sit on her bed.

"I never told you this Mila, but my father was a real jerk who preferred being drunk most of the time.

When I was about five, he hit my mother. It was over something stupid…I think she made chicken instead of beef. He slapped her face so hard that she flew across the room. That was the only time that she let him beat her. She warned him that next time, she would leave. That was followed by five blissful, happy, sober years, until my father was let go from his job. He drank himself stupid that day. By the time my mom got home from work, he was in a rage. My four-year-old brother and I pleaded with him to go to sleep and rest, but he just threw us like rag-dolls across the room. When he tried to take a swing at my mother, she was too quick for his sloppy, drunk hand and she escaped to her sister's house. That swing took him off balance and he collapsed to the floor where he spent the rest of the night while we joined my mother at our aunt's house.

"While we slept, my mother went back to our house and collected her things. She woke me up in the middle of the night to say goodbye, and told me that she would be back for my brother and me in one year. She made me promise that I would look after my brother while my father was getting help, and then she left. My father never drank again, but my mother never returned to him. For a year, my brother and I were shuttled between my father and my aunt, both of whom expected me to behave like an adult when I was just ten years old. I went to school and got good grades because I had made a promise to my mother. Then I would come home where I babysat my brother, and managed to cook and clean."

"Where was your mom all that time?"

"Working, sometimes at two or three jobs. She would send money to my aunt for necessities until she had enough money set aside to bring my brother and I to the States."

"And your father? Do you speak to him?"

"I do, a few times a year when I go back to Trinidad. He remarried, but it's beside the point. I just wanted to let you know that I know from personal experience that we are guided by primitive instincts. There are strong people and there are weaklings; if you don't set the rules, then you will be ruled. And certainly in relationships, there is one person who dominates the other...I will never be the dominated one."

I stare at my friend, noticing for the first time how her sunny disposition is clouded by the memories of this childhood trauma. I follow my instinct to give her a hug that most likely takes her by surprise, but to which she doesn't object. We stand in the quiet embrace— Michelle is still half-dressed and I am in my pajamas. We are women who are not afraid to lay our feelings bare to each other, but we have dressed our expectations of love in completely different outfits. I listen to my friend's breathing and I shake my head in agreement to her explanation of how things should work between two people. I agree, knowing that her experience will never let her give in to a love where both people are equal: one that doesn't require a ruler, but is fair; a love that doesn't demand constant control, but allows for total surrender. I know that such love is possible and for the same reason, I like Leo, against all common sense and reasons laid out by my friend. Michelle pats my hand, signaling that she has had enough of my embrace.

"OK, that is enough of this unnecessary, mushy crap. I just wanted you to know why I am so against being head over heels about a man. Now you do, and I hope you make the right decision."

"I believe I will."

"C'mon, go get dressed. I wanna beat the crowds," she urges me.

We get to IKEA in Red Hook in no time. We follow the orderly directions of arrows on the floor that guide us through beautifully set up rooms. I glance at my phone and sigh loudly enough for Michelle to hear.

"Leo still didn't call or text?"

I shake my head no, and look away to avoid a concerned look from my friend. I feel her reassuring squeeze of my elbow and I know that she is not judging me for my unexplainable feelings towards Leo.

"We have to go out for a drink tonight, to cheer you up. We haven't had a girl's night in a while," Michelle suggests.

"Good idea. I am in need of a good drink."

"Oh, look how cute these are! These glasses will go perfectly with Rob's dishes. Ooooh and these are even cuter!" Michelle completely gives in to the organized abundance of dishes and glasses and I can, for the first time, imagine my friend as a woman who cares about her man even though she would never admit it to herself. It takes us forty minutes to finish in the dish department; my phone is still silent. When we walk through the rows of plants, I pick out a small, fat cactus just to occupy my hands with something and to avoid constantly looking at my phone.

"Why did you get this ugly thing?" Michelle wrinkles her nose in disgust. "All these beautiful orchids and you found this…I am seriously starting to worry about your taste, Mila."

"It is cute. So what if it is prickly? It is just protecting itself, and did you know that cacti bloom? You just have to take care of them correctly," I say adoringly about my pudgy purchase.

"Whatever you say, girlfriend. Let's get lunch; I like the view from the cafeteria."

"OK."

IKEA's large cafeteria is as orderly as the rest of the store. The floor is lined with arrows that guide the public in the proper direction towards the counter where Michelle and I pick up our trays and cutlery and then proceed along, passing neatly packaged desserts, yogurts, and appealing foreign drinks that call out to my hungry taste buds. We decide to get the full Swedish experience and order Swedish meatballs, crepes with lingonberry and a pear fizzy drink. We plant ourselves in front of a panoramic view of New York city overlooking the Statue of Liberty, making our lunch even more appealing.

"I must say, this is one of the best views of the city. I love coming here just for that."

"Mgm!" Michelle agrees with a full mouth of meatballs.

"When I was a child, I always imagined her so much taller," I look in the direction of Lady Liberty, "and I was deeply disappointed as a teenager by the size of the White House. Have you been to D.C.?"

Michelle nods, still enjoying her meatballs. "I think it is done on purpose."

"What?"

"The way we receive certain images. Like the White House, for example. It is the most important house in the country...I don't think it will ever be portrayed true to size. It is meant to bring forth a feeling of patriotism, so it is better if it looks as grand as possible. And as for her, she is a symbol of hope and liberty; I am sure to most she looks bigger than her true size."

"Do you think it is the same way that we see some people?"

"Absolutely! Have you ever watched some politicians? They appear so authoritarian and confident that you never really think of their height, but then they show a group picture of some of the world leaders, and you see how the most confident leaders are the shortest people. It is fascinating! The same goes for actors—some leading men are not blessed with height, but you would never know it from watching their presence dominating the screen."

"I have noticed that. Even in the hospital, there are some people who take up the whole room with their personality, but then there are those who make you feel grand and important...You know what I mean?"

"How does Leo make you feel?"

"It's hard to explain." I pause, thinking of the words that would describe everything that my mind and body is experiencing. "I feel peaceful, hopeful when I'm with him. I feel he is himself with me and I don't feel I have to hold back how I am around him." There is also this churning heat of desire that I never felt with anybody else - I want to tell her, but decide to keep that to myself and instead add, "I can imagine a future with him: family, kids, and growing old."

"Mila, this guy really turned a love switch on in you. I just hope he is being truthful. I would hate for you to be hurt."

I look at my phone again, which shows that I have service, but still no call or a text from Leo. "I will give him a chance, but don't worry, I am not a complete idiot who would hang on to a guy who is an asshole."

We finish our IKEA lunch. Michelle drops me off at home and leaves to show Rob all the things that she bought for his apartment. We re-schedule our drinks for next time. The IKEA trip turned out to be a tiring shopping experience. I pick up the folder with the letters to continue reading about the relationship of two young people in love at a time where their future was so uncertain. When I look for the next set of letters, a small picture falls out that I have not seen before. It is a black and white portrait of a man in military uniform. He is young and handsome. His officer's hat is playfully cocked to the side and a Superman-like curl of hair is peeking from an otherwise slicked back do. I assume it is Jacob: he almost looks familiar—I feel like I have seen this face before, but shake off that feeling, thinking it is probably my imagination playing tricks on me. I stare into his eyes and even though the picture only has two colors, I can see that they are very light and full of life. I put the picture back gently into the folder and start reading the letter.

January 29ᵗʰ, 1941

I am so hungry, Jacob! The hunger is consuming every second of my existence. I dream of food; I smell the food as if it is being cooked in the kitchen. I hallucinate that I am tasting the sweetness of fruit. My aunt and I have been taking turns going to the store to get our rations, but she is becoming increasingly weak. Her wrinkled face is now smooth and shiny from edema; our legs can barely carry the weight of our dystrophic bodies… they do not listen. My body is so weak and tired. I feel as though I am floating above it all. I see, I smell, but I cannot move. I lay still, so very still, that one might think I am dead.

Aunt Olya sent me out to scavenge through the apartments of neighbors who had entrusted her with keys before they were able to escape Leningrad. It was eerie to go through the rooms frozen in time—most of the furniture was left behind. I carried wooden chairs down to my apartment to burn in the burzhuika. I was lucky to find some oil paint…we learned it can be eaten. In the apartment of the Bruner's, I scraped some spilled buckwheat off of the shelves and found a can of sardines in oil under the stove; it probably fell when they were evacuating. We made soup with it, and what soup it was! It warmed our bodies. It was liquid hope, and we made it last for a week.

One of the apartments was turned into a makeshift morgue by the Peysins. There is only Lena and Manya left. The rest of the family: grandmother, mother, father, and their little brother are all dead and the girls are too weak to take them to the morgue. Manya is going mad with grief from miscarrying her baby at seven months and she hasn't had any letters from her husband in months. None of us are getting any letters. I don't even know if you will ever be able to read mine. I don't know if I will have the courage to send them once the postal office opens. But these letters are the only connection I have to you. Each letter, each word, each sentence—they make me endure. So, I will keep writing. This letter is finished. Time to go to sleep and then start writing again. Good bye, Jacob! Love you always, yours, Iskra.

I put the letter away into the folder and start working on the growing pile of junk mail; I pause at an envelope that doesn't seem to contain either. The envelope is plain white with my address written in sharp, even handwriting; the return address is not indicated. I shake it to see if there is any object inside and put it to the light, but it seems that only a piece of paper is residing in the peculiar envelope. I open it carefully, subliminally fearing that I will release something dark with any sudden movement.

He is mine! Today I will seal my fate with his forever, and nothing and no one will stand between us.

The ominous words send chills throughout my body. I dial Leo frantically only to hear his voicemail. My mind runs through the scenarios of how this person will "seal" her fate with Leo's, and I feel all but helpless in preventing this hostile takeover of my own fate.

I decide to take the letter down to the local precinct where I am advised to write a report and that someone will contact me regarding it at some point. The lack of urgency shown by the police officer behind the plexiglass frustrates me. I am told that there is nothing I can do about Leo's sudden disappearance.

"If every girl filed a missing person's report on a boyfriend that they couldn't reach, we would need a much bigger police force," the officer chuckles under his breath. However, I must look pitiful enough because the officer softens his tone and enters Leo's information into the system. He assures me that if something comes up about him, I will be contacted.

I take an Uber to Leo's apartment where to my horror, I find yellow police tape guarding a puddle of dark blood that has soaked into the floor near the door to his apartment. I knock on the door, but only silence greets me. I knock again, hoping to hear any sound of stirring. The stirring comes, but it's from the neighbor's apartment. An elderly woman cracks her door open and looks me up and down, before softly whispering.

"What are you doing here, my dear?"

"Hi! I am looking for Leo—Dr. Renner. He and I work together and today, I couldn't get hold of him. Do you know what happened here?" I ask and hear my voice trembling, fearing what might be the answer.

"There was so much commotion! I couldn't see much. There were so many firemen and policemen and the ambulance people, going back and forth all day, all they told me was that someone was hurt. But who, I wouldn't know."

"Thank you," I tell the woman and when she closes the door, I am left to think in silence as to what I should do next.

I decide against talking to Michelle...I have bothered her enough with my drama, so I head to my parents' apartment to take my mind off Leo's troubling disappearance, and the bloody stain by his apartment door.

My mother opens the door and her look of happiness to see me changes into deep concern.

"Mila, my goodness, what happened? You look sick!" She touches my forehead with the back of her hand to check my temperature. When her motherly internal thermometer tells her that I am not ill, she ushers me into the kitchen. My parents' apartment is a cozy, three-bedroom unit located in a high-rise near Brighton Beach. Its walls are permeated with the smell of baked pies and borsch. My grandmother's presence lingers throughout in knitted, crocheted, and needle-pointed chair pillows, as well as tablecloths and towels. The familiarity of the surroundings brings instant comfort to my tormented mind.

I know my mother will pour me a cup of tea, a medicine that treats all ailments—physical and emotional—according to her.

"Geez Mom! Hi! Love you too!" I schlep straight to the kitchen and plop myself on the seat at the table that is always designated for me. My mom silently trails behind me and puts the teapot on to boil. Once the whistle of the pot notifies us that the hot water is ready, she swiftly pours it over the teabags in our cups. She moves a little dish that's always full of candy in between us.

"Where is Dad?" I hope he is not home—I don't want him to hear about my relationship drama, at least not yet.

"Oh, he went to sauna with his friends."

"How is work? How do you like it? Is it everything you imagined?" She inquires with general questions, trying to feel me out as to what has caused the turmoil of emotions making me look sick.

"It's fine…Yes, I love it." I give her general responses, still wondering if I should tell her about Leo.

"How is Michelle? Are you girls getting along?" My mother keeps probing.

"She is good; she's spending a lot of time with Rob."

"So, what is it, Mila? You don't look yourself. You tell me everything is fine, but something is really bothering you. Tell me! I am starting to worry." My mother finally loses her patience and demands an explanation.

"I don't know if I should worry you with this, but…" I pause and my mother picks up my dropped thought and takes charge of the conversation.

"Of course, Mila—you can tell me anything. I know I can be a crazy, overbearing mother sometimes, but it all comes from a place of love." She places a soft kiss on my head and pushes unruly curls behind my ears.

"I met someone," I almost whisper.

I hear my mother gasp at my surprise revelation.

"When? Who is he? What happened? Did he hurt you?" She bombards me with questions.

The questions overwhelm the emotional wall that was barely holding up, but it now caves in, collapsing and releasing a flood of tears and sobbing. All I manage to do is shake my head, no.

"Shhhh, shhhh." My mother rushes to my side, hugging my head, kissing it slowly and pressing it into the softness of her belly. "It is all right. Everything is going to be all right, my angel. Calm down, and tell me what has happened."

When the initial cascade of emotions subsides and I am finally able to speak, I tell her about Leo.

"He is a physician at my hospital and we have been seeing each other. Everything was going so well, but then, he just disappeared." The sobbing erupts again as I finish my sentence.

"What do you mean, he disappeared?" Concern grows in my mother's voice.

"He has a stalker and she wrote a strange note to me, and since then, I haven't been able to reach him. There is blood near the door to his apartment, and police tape." My body shakes through the sobbing that I cannot control.

"Shhhh, shhhh…It's OK. It's OK to cry. You cannot be so stoic all the time. Did you go to the police?" I only manage to nod yes while blowing my nose.

"They didn't want to do anything. They just told me to write a report and maybe someone will contact me tomorrow. But I am worried…What if tomorrow is too late? What if something bad happened to him?"

"Why don't you stay here at home tonight? I will cook something for you. You will feel better and we will go to the police together again tomorrow." My mother's comforting works, and the watershed of tears finally ceases. My body shakes with just an occasional sob.

We stay quiet for some time, my mother standing over me, consoling me as if I were a little girl.

"I want to go home. I just didn't see you for a few days and with everything that's going on with Leo, I just needed to speak to you. Thank you for listening." I squeeze her waist tightly. We stay still, both enjoying our embrace.

"Mama, I am scared," I whisper.

"Of what, Mila?"

"Of the way I am feeling: it is too much; I wasn't ready for it," I admit to her.

"Angel…No one is ever prepared. There is a lot you are experiencing right now, so many feelings and emotions, and because you are so inexperienced, it is completely overwhelming for you. You must understand something: when you love someone, you will feel a whole lot. Love is not perfect because humans make mistakes. I feel guilty that dad and I—we always acted happy around you; we hid our fighting from you, and never argued when you were in the same room. I think that gave you a false image of our relationship. I am sorry for that." My mother's confession leaves me confused.

"You and Dad argued?" My mother's admission turns the picturesque painting of their marriage into an abstract, mind-confusing dilemma.

"Of course!" She pulls away and looks straight into my eyes. "I broke quite a few dishes in the heat of an argument; many doors were slammed. But your father, bless his soul, was always charming. He would just hug me and make me talk and sometimes we would talk for hours, ironing out the imperfections of our relationship. We would never go to sleep until everything was resolved. I love your dad, but I don't always like him, and that is OK…That is life."

"I was thinking of breaking it off with Leo actually, because of this stalker complication, but now I am even more confused than before."

"How about you go and get some rest. Tomorrow, we will go to the police department together...People don't just disappear. We will find him and you will give him a chance to explain. Everybody deserves that." She bestows her motherly wisdom onto me, sealing it with a kiss on my forehead.

"You are right, Mama. I will call you tomorrow, OK? Don't tell Dad about this yet. I don't want him to worry."

"Of course, honey," my mother says agreeably.

I order an Uber which arrives in a few minutes; my mother walks me to the door and gives me another long and tight hug.

"Remember: it is OK to feel. You cannot control everything. You need to let the emotions in, even when they are not the ones you are used to feeling. I love you. Call me tomorrow, OK?"

I nod yes, leaving her house feeling slightly better.

When I get home, the apartment is quiet. I make myself a sandwich and immerse myself back in the time of the Leningrad blockade, and the suffering of WWII.

My dearest Iskra,

Please do not cry. I hate to see you sad. I am writing this letter because I feel that I need to be prepared for the inevitable. I need to tell you that when I die, I will be thinking of you. You are the spark that keeps me warm.

We are being exterminated and I hear bullets pass by me as I write this letter. It won't be too long before one finds me. I made arrangements for you to receive my personal belongings.

You were always stronger than me. I know you will make it through and I will watch you succeed and live a full life. I will see you at the end of each dusk, the touch of the last sunlight will be my kiss goodnight. I love you, Iskra!

~

February 15th, 1944

Hello my love! My Jacob,

I am writing this letter for the abyss. I now know that you will never read it. I will never feel your lips on mine. I will never hear your voice calling my name. My heart breaks, my chest hurts, and it is hard to breathe.

A man came to visit me—a man whose face I can't remember. He was dressed in black; he could have been death himself. He told me he served with you and that you made a pact that if one of you dies, the other will deliver the belongings to the person they cared about. He saw you shot directly in the head, so he followed the pact. He even brought me your shoulder straps, so the enemy can't use your death for their propaganda. I didn't get his name. I now have your letters…how funny; we have been writing to each other without the ability to send those letters.

I still sense your presence. At times, it is a feeling that I will hear the doorbell ring and you will be standing there with a bouquet of my favorite tulips. I walk the streets of Leningrad ruins and imagine I will see you on a bench near my home, patiently waiting for me. But all of this is no more. A week has passed since he came by, only now have I the strength to write to you my final letter.

204

Somehow, I hoped that we would make it through, that we would outwit death itself; that we would be the lucky ones. How naive my dreams were. This war took away so much from me, from the Soviet people, and from Russia! I can imagine the whole motherland is weeping with tears of blood.

Goodbye, my love, until the next dusk! Yours, always, Iskra.

My eyes tear up on learning the fate of the relationship between Jacob and Iskra. They were just young souls starting out their lives. How tragic their love story turned out to be. *Grandma, are you looking down at me? Are you happy? Am I making you proud?* I have so many questions that will forever stay unanswered.

CHAPTER 16

The sound of waves wakes me up. The morning light peeks through the curtains. I look at the screen on my phone, but am disappointed to find no messages from Leo. I hope I will be able to get some information today from the police. I drag myself out of bed, put on my scrubs, and head to the kitchen to have breakfast. Michelle is off today—she probably stayed at Rob's. I eat my instant oatmeal and head out the door to catch the train.

Outside, it is already humid and hot. A few minutes' walk later, I am at the train station which is packed with early risers who are heading to work. We all jam into the train car when it arrives, and the express ride delivers me to the city in thirty minutes.

The sign-out is straightforward and I begin to see my patients right away.

"Oh, hi guys! Sorry for interrupting. I am Dr. Roth." I introduce myself to a couple who are passionately kissing. My patient is Amy, a twenty-one-year-old, who presented with fever and vomiting. It still takes them a few seconds to finish their embrace after I introduce myself. When I finally get to see their faces, they both appear disheveled. Their shoulder length hair is greasy and hasn't been brushed for days; their clothes have been worn just as a necessary cover and not as a fashion statement; multiple holes of various sizes gape, unashamed of their existence. My patient's long-sleeved shirt is obsessively being pulled down so only her fingers are visible. The man, who I assume is her boyfriend, stays by her side, their hands interlocked.

"Hi, I am Brian, and this is Amy. She needs your help," he says in a raspy voice, shuffling his weight from one foot to another. I now notice that Amy's boyfriend is also sniffling; his eyes look wild with pinpoint pupils, and they dart back and forth as droplets of sweat collect on his forehead. Amy keeps her head down and doesn't make eye contact with me.

"I see you have reported a fever since last night? When we measured it here it is 102.7, that is pretty high. Are you feeling anything else, like nausea, abdominal ache, headache, muscle or joint pain, or sore throat?" I go through the usual line of questions, trying to figure out what might be the cause of her fever. Amy continues to stay quiet and Brian answers all of my inquiries instead.

"So, can you help her, doc, or what?" He shifts his weight back and forth impatiently, standing close to Amy's bed. "Just give her something for the fever so we can go."

"I cannot give her something for the fever because I don't know what is causing it yet. I need to examine her first," I snap at him. "You can wait in the waiting room; I will call you once I am done," I suggest to him so I can examine my patient without him standing guard. Unexpectedly, Amy starts sobbing and lifts up the sleeves of her shirt. Her skin is bruised and covered in scratches and signs of needle tracks. Both areas where the forearm joins the upper arm reveal several masses, bulging under the skin.

"It is all right baby, it is all right. She will help you… they will fix you right up." Brian kisses Amy on her forehead, not letting go of her hand. Now the beads of sweat are running down his face and I notice a tremble of his free hand.

"When did you last use?" I now speak directly to Brian.

"It is none of your damn business. We are here so you can fix her." He nods in the direction of Amy. "She needs me here, so I am staying."

"OK, Amy—please look at me. I need to examine you. Do you want Brian to stay for the exam?"

"Yes," is the only sound she graces me with. A quick direct eye contact from underneath her greasy locks darts to Brian to seek his approval. I glove up and go right for the lumps that Amy has exposed. They are soft, red, and hot to the touch.

"You have an infection under your skin. It can be very dangerous because it may lead to septicemia. It is a life-threatening blood infection. I will start you on antibiotics and you will be seen by an infectious disease doctor so we can take blood cultures and figure out which particular bacteria are causing your infection."

Amy looks up nervously at Brian, seeking the explanation for what my words mean in terms of their existence. He takes in a long sniffle before saying, without hidden annoyance: "How long exactly is this going to take?"

"She is going to be admitted and will stay until her infection is treated."

Amy lets go of Brian's hand and with a sigh falls back on the pillow and closes her eyes. Silent tears fall down her cheeks.

"Baby, baby—please don't cry. I just need to go for a minute, but I will be right back. You know…You understand. I can't stay, but I will be back." He covers her face in kisses.

"Please don't go. If you love me, stay with me," she begs softly.

"I love you baby girl, and I will be right back. I promise."

"I love you too," she whispers and nods, giving him permission to leave.

He wastes no time and dashes out of the room, abandoning the girl he claimed to love.

"How long have you been together?" I change the topic of conversation hoping that Amy will talk more now that Brian is not here.

"A year," she admits in a barely audible voice.

"And how long have you been using?"

"Three."

"Would you like to speak to someone about stopping?" I make a gentle suggestion.

"No. Brian, he, he is not ready yet." Even in her predicament, Brian is still the primary concern.

"Are you ready?" I press her about her life choices.

"You wouldn't understand. He loves me; he is the only one I have left. We can't…I can't be without him. We are together in this." She voices the logic of their codependent relationship.

"But you understand that both of you are putting your lives at risk. It seems to me that the drug you are using will always take precedent. Look…he couldn't wait to get out to get his next hit and it didn't matter that you needed him."

Amy starts sobbing again. "You don't understand. Just let me be. Give me the medication so I can get out of here," she demands.

I sigh, frustrated that I cannot get through to this young woman. Even imminent death doesn't scare her away from continuing on her self-destructive path.

"I will come back to check on you again, OK?" She looks away, still avoiding eye contact.

I leave her be and head to the computer so I can put in the orders for antibiotics, an infectious disease consult, and medications to prevent her from withdrawal symptoms.

"Have you spoken to the lovebirds?" Dr. White comes up to me as I am charting. "I saw them in the waiting room: they couldn't keep their hands off each other."

"Yeah, drug addicts…The girl is the patient. I'm just putting the orders through to treat her infection."

"Funny how people find each other and call it love."

"Love is blind, is what they say," I reply to Dr. White. As usual, she looks like she just walked off the pages of a magazine advertising medical uniforms. Her scrubs are of light grey fabric and not the usual green that is given out by the hospital; the cut is tailored perfectly to fit her figure. Her blond hair is tousled into perfect beach waves and her makeup applied so well that it only accentuates her features, without unnecessarily standing out.

"Can one really call a relationship where you completely lose yourself to be loved? Is it love when your whole existence is defined by the other person? I find it to be disturbing, but who am I to speak about love. I am on my third husband and thinking of upgrading," she giggles, but to me her laughter sounds sad. I force a giggle myself so she doesn't feel embarrassed by her admission.

"Oh well, Dr. Roth…Finish up here, and let's move on."

We are interrupted by a commotion originating from the waiting room. A flailing patient on a gurney is rolled in surrounded by several EMTs and a hospital security guard. An older gentleman, who introduces himself as the father of the violent patient, trails nervously behind. Dr. White and I jump in and try to assist so we can strap the patient down. The young man is short and skinny but his strength overpowers all seven of us, and he is able to kick one guard so hard that he falls to the floor.

"What the hell is he on?" Dr. White shouts to the father.

"Nothing, for the past three days. He is a habitual Xanax user, but decided to go cold turkey and stopped altogether. He first started to get paranoid and then violent. I brought him in when he tried to crawl on the walls," his dad says, almost crying, as he observes his son foaming at the mouth and fighting all of us with almost inhuman strength.

"God damn it! I need an IV access right now. He is not responding to intramuscular antipsychotics." Dr. White screams out for more help when injections into the patient's leg fail to subdue him.

Two more security guards join in and we are able to restrain the patient long enough to get the IV and push a paralytic agent. Finally, his body goes limp and I get to intubate him because now he can't even breathe on his own. When we finish with the patient, Dr. White and I face the patient's father who has been quietly sobbing, covering his mouth with his hand. The man is in his fifties; his hair is completely grey with a receding hairline, enlarging his already prominent forehead. A small round belly sits prominently between his narrow shoulders. His outfit of a plaid shirt and jeans with suspenders gives away the dad in him from a distance.

"This is my boy. How could this have happened? He was a straight A student, a star athlete. How could this have happened?"

"I am sorry, Mr.—?" Dr. White interrupts the difficult questions to which he may never receive answers. As a parent, he will forever bear the guilt of failing his child. Solace would only be found in his son's recovery.

"Mr. Vater...Johnny is my son."

"We need to transfer Johnny to ICU. He will stay intubated there for a few days until his condition stabilizes," Dr. White informs Mr. Vater.

"Of course, of course—please do everything that is necessary. It all started innocently enough with pot, but then he developed anxiety and started experimenting with street drugs. We tried interventions; we tried rehab twice, but he would just go back to the pills as soon as he got home." Mr. Vater tries to seek absolution, but all we can do is hear him out as to how Johnny started down the path that led him into the hospital.

"I am sorry…All that matters now is for him to get well enough; then we will try to offer him help. I hope he will be ready to accept it. Dr. Roth, come and find me if you need my help, but for now, arrange for Johnny to be transferred to ICU."

I examine our subdued patient and notice scrapes and bruises on both his hands. One cut on the right hand is particularly deep, and I am concerned for the swelling that is setting in—his silver Claddagh ring is already cutting into the skin of his ring finger. I call for the ICU fellow to come down and accept the patient, and ask if ICU may have the ring cutter in their supply room. I am told that they do, so I head upstairs to get it.

The elevator delivers me to the fifth floor: a distant planet called the intensive care unit or ICU within the vast galaxy of hospital care. The hallway is lit by the kind of lights that manage to make everyone look tired, and the smell of sterility is intoxicating, but there is also the sweet scent of something that I cannot distinguish. This is where patients come for their last chance to be saved. The sound of life-saving machines doesn't attract my attention anymore…it is now the white noise of my life.

Two nurses sit quietly, observing the monitors which relate how patients are doing through the peaks and valleys of their cardiac activity. An exhausted looking ICU resident is glued to the screen of his cellphone, his head drops and then jumps up as he is startled awake again from a brief slumber. He looks up, and furrows his brows. He is probably confused by my presence on his floor.

"I need a ring cutter," I explain. He points in the direction of the supply closet and returns to his cellphone screen.

I turn the corner and head to the end of the hall-way to reach my destination. I pass rooms with patients lying still, connected to wires and tubing like puppets, their life systems managed by others. A familiar name on one of the doorways elates my spirit. I touch the shell calculator in my coat pocket, and walk in to say hello to Mr. Katz.

The room is filled with balloons, and people all looking down somberly at a small person hidden within blankets and wires. Mr. Katz doesn't stir; his eyes are closed, and his mouth is open with no sound of breathing escaping his dry lips. A middle-aged woman whimpers quietly in the corner, three men huddle together near the edge of the bed. A few nurses stand next to the patient's bed, with ICU attending closely monitoring the screen, making sure the patient is not in distress...I realize that they are saying goodbye. The rhythmic drumming of his heart, sounded off by the cardiac monitor, turns into a long, deafening beep. My impulse to start CPR is halted by the memory of his chart: do not resuscitate, do not intubate. His wishes were clear and are respected, but it doesn't stop me from choking up on a ball of rolled up sadness and helplessness. I touch my shell calculator again, saying a quiet thank you to the man I was fortunate to know.

I exit the room, not attracting anyone's attention. I grab what I came for and with my head hanging low, make my way back to the ED. I have to go on.

Once Johnny's finger is free from the constriction of the ring, I make a mad dash to the cafeteria. I swallow my salad, chewing it just enough so I don't choke. I wash it down with black, sweetened coffee hoping it will give me a boost of energy to last the rest of the day. I have to finish the cup on my way to the bathroom. I am about to leave when I hear sobs coming from the last stall. I bend down to look under the door, and spot ER green scrubs and familiar sneakers.

"Dr. Bryce? Are you OK?" I knock on the door. "This is Dr. Roth. Can I help you with anything?"

The sobbing stops and I hear the door being unlocked. I open it slowly when Dr. Bryce doesn't come out. I find her sitting on the floor in the corner of the stall. Her eyes are red and puffy from crying.

"Are you OK?" I repeat myself, surprised to find her having a breakdown.

She nods, wiping her face with a tissue and forcing a smile. "You are the last person I want to see right now."

"I heard you crying…I'm just checking on you. If you don't want to talk to me, that is fine. I will leave." Dr. Bryce stays quiet and I turn to leave.

"Wait, Dr. Roth! I am sorry! I have been a real bitch to you for no reason. I have just been really overwhelmed lately and Dr. Kramer has been on my case, you know?" I turn back and nod, acknowledging her apology. "And by the way, I have no feelings for Dr. Renner. I might have had a crush on him last year, but that is all over. I had no right talking to you the way that I did before." She plays with a crumbled tissue in her hands, keeping her gaze down.

"Apology accepted, Dr. Bryce," I tell her, sitting down on the floor next to her. The silence of the bathroom is somehow comforting. "Why have you been crying?"

"I don't know if I can do this," she reveals.

"Do what?"

"Emergency medicine." Dr. Bryce throws her head back and lets out a sigh of relief. "I cannot handle the stress of it all. I have been contemplating switching to psychiatry..." She pauses to hear my reaction.

"That's cool," is all I can tell her, not knowing how to react to this revelation.

"It has been weighing on me, this decision. On one hand, I can be done in another year and then start practicing emergency medicine, or do I drop out and lose two years waiting for a match to a psych. program?" She gives voice to a question that only she can answer.

"Well, in one year, you can do what you hate for the rest of your life, or in two years, you can start doing what you will love for the rest of your life. That's how I would look at this." I offer my opinion.

"I guess you're right...I have to start thinking that way. Thank you, Dr. Roth." Dr. Bryce's soft tone is unusual to hear. I smile at her and rub her shoulder. Our pagers go off at the same time, telling us that there is another arrival that needs our attention. We get off the floor and rush out of the bathroom towards ER.

"This guy was found just a few blocks over passed out with a needle still in his arm. Five Narcans did nothing," a short, Hispanic EMT with slicked back curly hair and a clean-shaven face reports as he wheels in a patient from the dock. His partner, a rosy cheeked, pudgy woman with blond hair pulled back in a tight ponytail is continuing to deliver chest compressions.

"Oh, my God—I know this guy! His girlfriend is in ER; he left her there just a few hours ago. What is his name? Brian, I think Brian," I announce to the people around me. No one looks up. It doesn't matter if I know him. We run the code for forty minutes, but our attempts to revive him are futile. Dr. White, who was called to run the code, declares the time of death. I go to visit Amy who is still waiting for a bed so that she can be moved to the medicine floor.

"Amy, I have some news about Brian." I sit down at the edge of her bed. "He was brought in by the ambulance a while back. He was found not far from here. He overdosed. We did everything we could. I am really sorry to tell you this, but Brian passed away." I take her cold, pale hand into mine and give it a light squeeze.

Amy's face contorts in pain and horror; her mouth opens, but no sound comes out. She thrashes in the bed, then jumps out of it, but shrieks in pain from the pull of the IV that is inserted into her arm.

"Amy stop…You will hurt yourself!"

"You are lying, you are lying! He cannot be dead!!! He promised to come back for me—he promised me!" She falls to the floor, brought down by the grief of losing her boyfriend. I call security to help me get her back into bed. Her crying now turns to a monotonous moan. "Take me to him," she pleads.

"I will, but you have to promise me that you will stay calm, otherwise, I will have to sedate you." Amy nods, agreeing to my condition.

I arrange for a wheelchair and take her personally to the room where Brian's body is still lying, his face covered by a bed sheet. I prepare Amy so she is not shocked by all the tubes and wires that are protruding from his orifices and his limbs.

I place the wheelchair so she is directly by Brian's face and leave her, letting her know that I'm right behind the door.

She calls for me about ten minutes later. Her eyes and nose are swollen and red, small capillaries have erupted over her cheeks from wiping the tears that were still running down her face, but now she isn't trying to stop the watershed.

"Do you want me to do anything for you? Call anyone?" I ask, but she shakes her head, no.

"Get me help; I want to get clean," she says with a loud confidence that I haven't heard from her before.

"OK, I will." I take her to the room and write additional orders for her to speak to a social worker so she can start the process of liberating herself from the drugs that hold her body and mind hostage. The death of Brian unchains her from the codependent relationship. Now, she has an opportunity to escape and I hope that she will run away—far, far away and never be trapped in the same prison of a relationship and drugs.

We sign out our patients to the next shift and I am glad that I will have the next two days off so that I can recover physically and emotionally from both the toll of the shifts, and the lack of news from Leo. Before I leave the hospital, I decide to stop on the floor where I know I will be recharged with hope. With my pass, I open secure double doors and breathe in the smell of baby skin and diapers. My feet take me to the room with the glass window overlooking the new life. Clear plastic bassinets are lined up containing the precious miracles that have just entered the world. What does the world have in store for them I wonder? There is hope in the new beginnings; I feel my soul settle into the cozy bundle of warm mush. I leave the hospital content, witnessing both death and new life within this grey building.

My parents will come to pick me up later so that we can go to the police department together. I hope I can find out what happened with Leo.

CHAPTER 17

My mom calls to tell me that they will head out in an hour to come get me. I stop by the Chinese food restaurant near my place in case they are hungry. A skinny young teenager takes my order and disappears while I sit down at one of the tables. I stretch out my feet and close my eyes.

"Miss, miss—your order is up," the young man shakes me awake.

I rub my eyes, surprised that I've dozed off in this hot and noisy place. "Thank you!" I pay the bill and leave with the bags of food. The humidity has gotten worse since the morning. I am sweaty and tired, and strands of hair are sticking to my face. I finally get to my building and drag my feet up the stairs to the apartment. I fumble to find the keys and as I step into the dimly lit corridor, I see a figure sitting by my apartment door, slouched over with his head on his knees. The figure stirs and I recognize the familiar features.

"Leo?! Where were you?!" I drop the bags of food, run, and shake him out of his sleep. My voice breaks and tears flood my eyes. "Where were you?!" I involuntarily reach out and hit him, trying to hurt him for making me feel helpless, for worrying, and for not knowing what had happened to him.

He wakes, and wraps his hands around me tight. The hug prevents me from hitting him, but it only intensifies my sobbing. He lets go, grabs my hands and covers my palms in kisses, then presses my hands to his cheeks and stares into my eyes with a gaze of warm sunlight that looks incredibly sad.

"I am so sorry! I am so sorry that I disappeared. Laura tried to commit suicide and frame me for it. I was arrested and spent two days in a cell. As soon as I got out, I came right over."

"I was so worried, so angry at you! I didn't know what happened! I went to your place and saw blood on the floor and I thought something had happened to you!"

"I am sorry. I should have taken her more seriously." A nosy neighbor peeks at us through his door and I decide it would be better to take our drama inside the apartment. I open the door and we get inside.

Under the bright bulbs in the entryway of my apartment, I finally see how terrible Leo looks. He has the same clothes on from two days ago, but now they are covered in brown stains of dried blood. His beard has gotten longer and is messy; his red eyes have dark bags… he must have had a restless and stressful two days. The lines on his forehead and between his brows have gotten deeper. He looks older, and very tired.

"I am so happy you are OK." I place a soft kiss on his chapped lips. "You look terrible. Do you want to take a shower? I have Chinese, more than enough for both of us."

"I have nothing to wear."

"We have a washing machine in the apartment; I can throw everything in there."

"I must admit, in my state of exhaustion, your offer is quite tempting." Leo manages to smile.

"Bathroom is right there. Go."

Leo walks off to take a shower while I change and put the food on the table. The sound of water lets me know that I can go in and grab his clothes to throw in the washer. I knock on the door.

"I am going to grab your clothes!"

I walk in, keeping my head down, giving Leo some privacy while he is completely nude.

"Mila?"

"Yes?" I turn around and face Leo who has pulled back the shower curtain and is standing stark naked, droplets of water covering a body that is defined by firm muscles. I stretch out my hand and glide it down his warm skin. The spark of desire heats the depth of my belly. He doesn't have to say any words. I see the hunger burning in his eyes, recognizing that I long for his touch. I take off my clothes and climb in under the hot water, where the steam covers us in a warm blanket. Leo traces his fingers along my lips, then down my neck, his touch is soft and raises goosebumps on my skin. His hand travels to my breasts, where he pauses, a moan escapes my lips letting him know not to stop. His hands circle my nipples and continue the journey to my belly, he pauses again.

"Are you sure?" he murmurs.

"Yes." And I sound so loud I surprise myself.

"Let me take you to bed," Leo manages to say in between our kisses. "Can you also undo your hair? I like it when you wear it down: it is like a waterfall of fire, and your eyes are of cold ice. You are a wild beauty, Mila."

We both get out and dry each other's bodies. I hand him my oversized plush robe which looks extremely small on him, with the sleeves barely covering half of his forearms; it overlaps just enough to cover his manhood. I giggle at the sight and send him off to bed promising to join him in a minute after I throw his clothing in the wash. I remove the blood with hydrogen peroxide, erasing the last physical presence of Laura, and start the washing machine. The food is tucked into the fridge…I don't know when we will eat. I give a quick call to my mother letting her know that Leo is here with me and promise to call her tomorrow to explain his disappearance.

I run to the bedroom and jump under the covers where I find Leo sleeping.

I place a soft kiss on his lips, deciding not to wake him after the torturous two days he's had, and just spoon with him, falling into a restful sleep.

The next morning, I am awakened by Leo nuzzling into the back of my neck. "Good morning, beautiful!"

"Morning! You fell asleep yesterday before we could finish up," I blame him lightheartedly.

"I am sorry, but we can start and finish now." He rolls me towards him, his erection obvious and unashamed, pressing against my belly.

"Morning sex is the best, especially now that we both have no place to be." He starts placing kisses on my face.

"About that…It is kind of embarrassing, but I've never had sex before, actually." I sink in under the covers awaiting Leo's reaction nervously.

He stops his kisses and sits up. "How is this possible? You are beautiful, smart, young—I didn't expect you to be a virgin."

"Well, I guess I just paid more attention to books than boys." I shrug my shoulders, reasoning why my virginity lasted past my teen years.

"Are you sure you want me to be your first man?" Leo asks cautiously.

"Never been more sure, but you seem to be… scared. Are you?"

He smiles softly. "I am quite honored. I am only scared that I won't deliver the best experience for you, but I am willing to try." He positions himself between my legs and starts a trail of soft kisses leading to the inside of my thigh where the warmth of my body has been waiting for his touch. Outside, the July weather gifts us a downpour: drops of water drum away against my window, cascading into a dance of unity and then separation, before they reach their destination, ultimately pooling into large puddles on the pavement.

We spend the whole morning in bed, with Leo sending my body into the highest peaks of ecstasy. Our bodies are hot and sweaty; I lie on my back as Leo towers over me. His thrusts become faster, and he leans over me, supporting his weight with his strong, muscular arms. His lips cover mine, my tongue reaches into his mouth. The vertex of desire tightens inside my belly; the pleasure erupts and the wave of it floods my senses. Leo grunts and presses his hips deeper against me and finally stills, achieving his release. He lays down on top of me…I feel my body relax and enjoy the sweet sensation of being tired from our love-making.

"I am hungry," I admit out loud.

Leo laughs loudly. "Yes, this certainly has worked up my appetite too."

We get up and get dressed. Leo still has to wear my robe while his clothes dry. I am glad Michelle is staying at Rob's so that we have the whole apartment to ourselves. Yesterday's Chinese food tastes absolutely amazing and we devour every little bit.

I sip from my large cup of coffee, thinking how my life all of a sudden changed course since I met Leo. Just a week ago, I thought that romance and everything that comes with it—the butterflies, the anticipation of the touch, the look from the other person that makes you get goosebumps, as well as optimism for the future— would not be a part of my life.

"What are you thinking about?" Leo questions my silence and reaches out for my hand.

"Nothing; I am just happy."

"You make me happy too," he admits, and he kisses the inside of my wrist. "I have to go home soon, tend to some emails, but remember—we have to be at my parents' tonight by eight. They have a small get-together planned for friends and family. I will pick you up at four because I want to take you to one of my favorite places by their house." He gets up, comes around and pulls me up towards him.

"Are you sure you want me to meet your parents?" I look directly into his eyes.

"I've never been more sure. God, you are beautiful!" He looks at my face and sinks his hand into the curls of my hair, drawing me in for a kiss.

"Go!" I send him away feeling that he will not be able to go unless I force him to. "I will be ready by four."

CHAPTER 18

At four o'clock sharp Leo calls my cell, letting me know that he is waiting for me downstairs. I grab the bouquet of peonies and a cake that I bought earlier and head outside. After much deliberation, I choose to wear a strappy white dress and platform beige sandals. I decide to complement the outfit with my grandmother's earrings and the bracelet of amber, and I keep my hair down, happy that the day is not humid.

Leo looks rested and he smiles when he sees me walking up to him. He is dressed in jeans and an untucked, short sleeve shirt of a deep turquoise color, matching the color of his car. He holds the door of his Camaro open for me with one hand and with the other one hugs my waist, pulling me towards him for a kiss. Our lips lock, unapologetic to the people around us.

"We have to get going," Leo breathes out as he holds my hand, guiding me into the low seat. "I have to warn you about my mother. She talks a lot and she can be inappropriate: she will ask you very personal questions. I have to apologize for that in advance." Leo gets into the car and we start to drive.

"Don't worry. I don't think anyone is more inappropriate than my mother. I can handle it. What do you want to show me?"

"There is a place, a park in Glen Cove. It's really nice, peaceful, right on the water. I stop by there when I visit my parents. I wanted you to see it tonight, before we are bombarded by all the people at the party."

At this hour, traffic is moving well through the winding Belt Parkway towards Long Island, with most people setting up for dinner or heading to the city for some Saturday night fun. We get to Glen Cove and the Camaro starts to climb up the narrow streets of the quiet town. We enter a small parking lot.

"We are here; let me help you," Leo offers before I can get out of the car. He opens the door for me and helps me to my feet. We walk out to the park entrance, holding hands. The place is covered in lush, green tall trees, and thin, twisting trails run up the hills on our right. In front of us, through the trees, behind a stage with white columns set in a semicircle, I see a thin stretch of sandy beach that is kissed by the calm waters that sparkle like starlight in the setting sun. Few beachgoers still lie out on the cooling shoreline, but the park looks incredibly peaceful. The air is fresh and light after this morning's rain.

We walk holding hands, me taking in the sounds and the view of the new place and Leo purposefully leading me somewhere up the picturesque trail. Once we reach the top of the small hill, I finally see why Leo wanted me to see this place. Here, large stone pillars that no longer have a roof to support draw you in to step inside what looks like an ancient ruin and take in the view. We sit on the edge of the wall, Leo leaning against the pillar and me settling in between his legs with my back resting against his chest. Behind us, large houses nestle between and on top of the boulders. In front of us, the water escapes into the horizon.

"It is a beautiful place...I am glad you brought me here." I snuggle against his firm chest that rises and falls steadily, and I can feel his heartbeat resonating through my body.

Leo buries his nose in my hair and takes a deep breath. "I am glad you like it," he says and I feel him smiling. "But I wanted to talk to you about something. I promised to be completely honest and I intend to be." He tenses up and wraps his arm tighter around my waist. "I told you about Laura and that she was a patient of mine. What I didn't tell you was that she was with my brother the night he overdosed. She was the one who called the ambulance before she herself passed out. Danny had been doing hard drugs for a while and I felt embarrassed, but at the same time helpless and guilty that I couldn't persuade him to stop. I told him during one of our last fights that if he overdosed, it would be better if he died than if I tried to save him. When it actually happened, I was crushed with remorse...I was in complete shock that what I predicted had occurred. I found comfort in speaking with Laura. I wanted to find out what my brother was going through before he died. In retrospect, I now feel that those few conversations started Laura's obsession with me, and that's why I was slow to initiate any kind of protective order against her—I felt guilty. I am sorry, for this situation has affected us. I truly hope that Laura's dark shadow is fleeting, and will not last. I want to make you happy because you make me want to be a better person. You look at me and I feel hope and balance: the calm that I never felt. It is like you are at the end of my search, and I didn't even know I was looking for you."

I turn around to face him and put my hands on his cheeks. The sun is reflected in Leo's eyes; they resemble the amber jewel I am wearing.

"You had good intentions. Laura was sick…She was not in her right mind. Don't fault yourself for what she did. We are safe. I am enjoying our 'now' and I am not dwelling on the past." I kiss his eyes and then softly, his lips.

"You are a strong woman, Mila; I love that about you. Let's go…My parents can't wait to meet you!"

"Do they know about Laura?" I want to know how much Leo has told his parents so I don't disclose more information than necessary. He shakes his head no.

"I didn't tell them. My parents went through enough worrying with Danny. I didn't want them to worry about me too," Leo explains.

"Where was Boss the two days that you were not home?"

"The kid who walks him lives just across the hallway. When all the commotion was happening with Laura, he happened to be home and he took Boss in."

"Oh, that's good," I sigh with relief. "I was worried about him too."

Leo smiles and breathes out a thank you, then draws me in for another kiss before we get into his car and take off to meet his parents.

We pull into the driveway in front of a craftsman style house with a beautifully manicured lawn, and flower boxes full of blooming pink and white flowers under the windows. Leo gives me a supportive nod and a wink and we get out of the car. Leo's mother - a petite, blond woman with a short haircut - greets us in a crescendo voice as we open the car doors to get out.

"Hello! Hello! Hello! There is our girl! Leo, she is beautiful! I am Leo's mother, Nina." She stretches her hand out for a shake, but then changes her mind and hugs me, planting two kisses on my cheeks. "I am so happy to meet you. Quite honestly, I was getting worried about my son...he's never brought a girl to meet us. I was starting to think he had other inclinations." She laughs loudly at her own joke.

"Mom, please don't embarrass me," Leo scolds.

"Oh shush, you!" She waves him off. "Come—kiss your mother. I haven't seen you in weeks!" she orders. Leo obliges, and plants a quick kiss on his mother's cheek.

"Nice to meet you! I am Mila." I introduce myself. "These are for you." I present her with my bouquet of peonies. "And here's a cake for dessert."

"You are a sweet child. I can tell that we will get along just fine. Come with me; I will introduce you to everyone."

"Leo, dear! Go help your father put the flowers into a vase and the cake in the fridge. Don't worry, I will make sure Mila is having fun." Without giving Leo a chance to object, she wraps her arm around mine and we walk off, Nina leading me into the backyard along a paved walkway on the side of the house. The backyard is fenced off by a tall white fence, and large pine trees alongside create privacy and seclusion. A stone patio by the back entrance is shaded by the gazebo, with leafy vines climbing up the pillars. A table underneath is loaded with trays of untouched food.

"This is my sister, Polina." Nina points to a woman who has long curly hair and an uncanny resemblance to Leo's mom. "She has three children. Ah, here they are: this is Kevin, Dean, and Alex." She introduces me to three young men in their twenties who look like triplet body builders. They nod to acknowledge my presence and return to chatting amongst themselves while sipping beer. "These are my good friends, George and Tamara, and also, my girlfriend, Sveta." She waves to her friend who is standing in the distance playing with a small child. "Her husband died last year," Leo's mother leans in to whisper into my ear and shakes her head as if in disbelief that such a person is no longer alive.

"I am sorry to hear that."

"Don't be sorry, he was a complete asshole. He gambled everything away, and turns out he had a love child—who is now fifteen—with some divorcee." She continues to share small secrets about everyone who is in attendance. We walk across the yard to the swing that has grapevines covering the roof. An older couple swings slowly while talking to a younger girl with short, pixie hair.

"And these are our neighbors, Alan and Elaine. And of course, their daughter, Jackie." I smile and shake everyone's hand.

"Come, I will show you my garden." She pulls me away from Jackie and informs me yet again in hushed tones that she used to pursue Leo when they were teenagers. But the poor girl didn't have a chance, so I don't need to worry about her. She is now engaged, and their family is invited to attend the wedding.

"Oh, I am not worried," I tell her confidently.

"I know. I knew when my boy met the right girl, it would be serious. Ahh! I am such a happy mother! So, this is my garden. I have roses over here, my vegetable garden over there, and my strawberries are in the back." She changes topics so fast that it is hard for me to even insert any reply. By the time words come out of my mouth, they are already out of place for the current conversation.

"This is beautiful."

"Yes, yes, it is. But come, I have to show you the inside of the house." She wraps her arm around mine and leads me inside.

The split-level house is charming. There is no opulence, but everything inside looks like it was picked out by someone with an eye for design. The house feels like a home, maybe because I know Leo grew up here.

"This is the living room, here is the kitchen, there is the office, and the bedrooms are upstairs." She leads me on a quick tour of the whole house and I can only say short, one syllable words such as wow, nice, and yes in between all her excited chatter.

"This is Leo; I think he is about nine months." She points to one of the pictures lining the wall of the staircase. Leo, a chubby baby with fat rolls on his arms and legs is laying on his tummy, pushing part way up, and lifting his head to smile at someone behind the camera. Fuzzy blond hair is just starting to cover his whole head, and I can see that the light in his eyes hasn't changed. The same blond, long lashes framed them then, as now. His smile is full of happiness.

"And this is him and his brother Danny when they were little. Danny died a few years ago. They were so close…Leo always looked after him." She pauses on the steps in front of the picture and I hear sadness in her voice. Although they are siblings from the same parents, Leo and Danny look nothing alike. Leo's blond hair is in complete contrast to Danny's straight, jet black locks.

In the next photo, Leo is now seven or eight. His blond locks are longer and lighter. He is dressed in a t-shirt and shorts; his brows are furrowed and his lips are pursed. He has his hand protectively wrapped around Danny's shoulder who is probably around four. He is dressed similarly to Leo: his head is covered by a fedora and his smile stretches from ear to ear.

"They are adorable," I tell Mrs. Renner as I take in the details of each picture.

"And here are the boys during their graduations from their high schools." She points to two separate pictures of the boys in their cap and gown. "They were both so smart. But Danny was always lucky—things just came to him easily. Leo always had to study; his face was always buried in some book." In the picture, Leo is a pimply teenager with awkward facial features that don't quite fit his face, and he doesn't yet look like the Leo I know now. The only constant feature is the light in his eyes.

Nina stands in front of the wall lined with pictures of her family. She proudly moves from face to face as memories flood her mind, and emotions project on her face. She pauses at the picture of little Leo giving Danny a protective brotherly hug. Her lips smile, but her eyes are full of sadness.

"Danny was such a sweet soul. He was always searching for a purpose for his existence. He had such plans, such capabilities, but he couldn't handle rejection. He wanted to create something and have everyone accept it and be happy. But he found people to be malicious and petty. When I asked him why he started taking drugs, he said, *It is like I am floating in a different universe, unburdened, Creator and creation— anything is possible there. This world has nothing for me; I am nothing in this world.* He didn't see himself. My precious boy, may you rest in peace." Her voice trembles, the words spoken reminding her of the loss that will forever send sharp pain through her motherly heart. "Mila, please forgive me." A forced giggle escapes her. "I am just so happy that Leo has you, please take care of him. He has a strong mind, but a gentle heart, although he doesn't always show it."

"I promise, Mrs. Renner, I will." I breathe out the words like a vow.

"Mom, did you forget that you have a house full of guests?" Leo appears at the bottom of the stairs and interrupts his mother's tour and our bonding. "Dad is looking for you."

"All right, all right. What does he need now, this man? I swear, I don't know what he would do without me. Mila, I still have more pictures to show you... maybe a little bit later." And she leaves me on the stairs with Leo.

"Did she overwhelm you? I know she can be a bit too much to handle." Leo walks up the stairs towards me, and stops a few steps below so that his face is directly in front of me. He stretches his hand and cradles my cheek lightly with his palm. I press against it, enjoying the warmth of his touch.

"Don't worry, she was fine, but I don't think I memorized everyone's name and I didn't meet your father yet," I admit to him, embarrassed.

"You will get to know them. Come, I will introduce you to my father." As if on cue, his father walks in from the backyard and heads towards us.

He is still a handsome man in his sixties. His raven hair is touched by grey, but only on his temples. His skin is tanned and he looks very physically fit.

"This is my dad, Michael." Leo stretches out his arm towards his father. "This is Mila." He wraps his other hand around my waist, drawing me closer and we walk downstairs.

"It is a pleasure to meet you. I hope my wife didn't scare you off with her non-stop chatter. Stay with Leo, and you might be safe." He smiles warmly at me. All three of us walk out to the backyard.

Leo repeats the names of all the guests. The evening weather is warm and pleasant with the sound of cicadas filling the air. Leo's mother and father keep checking to see that I am enjoying the night, and Leo is holding me by the waist tightly in case his mother tries to drag me away again. I chat with everyone about the general topics of weather and jobs and when all the food is finished and tables are cleared, the guests head out. Leo and I enjoy the quietness of the backyard after all the guests leave and his parents walk to the front to see everyone off. He doesn't need to tell me how he feels about me. I feel it in his gaze and his touch. The comfort of knowing adds to the bliss of the night. I lean my head on his shoulder and feel his lips softly kissing me.

"Did I tell you I love the smell of your hair?" Leo murmurs. "The wild spirals of fire." He smiles while wrapping one of the strands around his finger. "I am so happy in this moment. I feel at peace next to you." He lifts my chin and draws me in to give me a soft kiss on the lips.

"I feel it too," I whisper back. This man makes me feel something that I didn't understand before, a feeling I thought would pass me by. But here I am, bathing in the comfort of mutual attraction, and the pleasure of knowing that I am special to Leo as he is the only one for me.

"Ah, there you are you two love birds!" Leo's mother appears from the house with his father trailing behind her. "I was looking for you. I didn't get to show Mila your grandparents yet." She unceremoniously comes between us and we break our embrace to make room for her.

"Look Mila, these are my husband's parents." She points to the picture of a grinning-from-ear-to-ear elderly couple, somewhere on a sunny beach. "They live in Florida...wonderful, wonderful people. And these are my parents." She has several pictures in her hands, spanning several decades apart. "Did Leo tell you about my father? He really was a great man and so kind. He could fix anything. Here he is with Leo when he graduated from medical school."

237

"Oh, Leo showed me this picture." I admit having seen it before at Leo's place.

"Here he is holding Leo when he was about two." A faded color photo shows a still chubby Leo in only his diaper, frozen mid-jump onto his grandfather's lap. Both of them are overjoyed in that moment of silliness. "Here are my parents when they were still very young. I think they are attending someone's wedding. My mother died five years ago and my dad just last year." Leo's mother gently glides her hand across the picture of her parents and passes it to me to take a look.

A young woman with dark hair in a big up-do popular in the fifties is looking lovingly at Leo's young grandfather. The wide shouldered suit sits well on his slim figure. The injured eye is covered with a patch and he is wearing large glasses; the curls of his blond hair rebelliously fall on his forehead. I recognize the strong chin and jaw that Leo has inherited from him. But there is something else that looks so familiar about him—I have a nagging feeling that I have seen him somewhere before.

The amber eyes are clear and happy, the same color as Leo's eyes…The same amber that I have seen in my dreams. Could it be? I have to show Leo the picture.

"These are lovely - thank you for showing them to me." Leo's mother unexpectedly leans in and gives me a peck on my cheek and a quick hug.

"And how are your parents, Mila?"

"Oh, they are well. They live in Brooklyn."

"Where do they come from?"

"My dad is from Lvov and my mother emigrated from Israel, but she was born in Saint Petersburg."

"Do you speak any Russian?"

"No, unfortunately not," I say regretfully. "My parents had to learn English and practice it; I went to an English-speaking school and it was hard to keep up with learning Russian. But my parents still speak Russian to each other."

"Oh, their story reminds me of our experience. In order to learn English, we had to speak it as much as possible. I watched cartoons with Leo so I could learn, but I do regret now that I did not push Leo to at least learn conversational Russian."

"OK, Mom and Dad—thanks for having us, but we have to get going." Leo springs to his feet, helps me get up, winks, and gives a light squeeze of my hand.

"Oh, no! Already? But we didn't even have tea yet," his mother cries out sadly.

"Mom, I think everyone had at least three cups already," Leo reminds her.

"Oh shush…That doesn't count. We have to have a proper tea, sitting down, with some cake," she scolds him.

"Thank you, Mrs. Renner—I really appreciate it, but I am afraid that since I started residency, my bedtime is an early one."

"That's right! I remember when Leo was a resident… he was exhausted all the time. What are you waiting for?" She nudges her son. "Mila needs rest; you have to leave now." Leo just rolls his eyes at his mother's turn-around and we say goodbye to his parents with his mother insisting that we come visit them very soon.

We walk towards Leo's car hand in hand, with my head resting comfortably against his shoulder. Until recently, we were just a couple of strangers, but now we walk the walk of two people falling for each other.

Leo's car swiftly gets us on the highway.

"Did you enjoy your time?" Leo asks me, gently squeezing my knee.

"I really did," I tell him sincerely.

"Why don't you stay at my place tonight? I like waking up next to you." He gives me the smile of a satisfied man.

"I loved it too, and I can stay—I'm off tomorrow." I take his hand off my knee and kiss his palm.

"But stop by my house first. I'll grab some clothes and I want to show you something." A suspicion that I am right about my discovery is growing stronger the more I try to remember the details of the photographs. This would be an unbelievable coincidence. Grandmother, is this your work from above?

I leave Leo waiting in the car double-parked on the other side of my building. Dark clouds cover the pre-dusk sky, and wind forms miniature dust tornadoes on the asphalt. I make a mental note to grab an umbrella on the way down: it will surely start to pour any minute. I dash up to the apartment, not waiting for the elevator, and quickly grab a change of clothing and my grandmother's box. In my rush to get back to Leo, I lose hold of the box and it falls on the floor, its precious cargo sent sprawling. I carefully place everything back inside and when I stack the letters, my eyes catch a glimpse of a white sheet of paper folded into four. It bears my name in a familiar handwriting.

Mila,

When you are reading this letter, I will no longer be around. But I wanted to leave something that will help you when you are struggling, and there is no light to give you hope.

My angel, you have to know in the darkest of hours, in the desperation so hopeless that life seems worthless, at that very moment, you have to tell yourself: one more breath, one more blink of an eye. You say that to yourself and force your mind to continue to smolder; it will keep the life force pumping through your body long enough until a change will be able to ignite the spark of life back to fire, burning so hot and so high that death will back away far into the darkness it came from.

I lived a long life; some may say it was a hard life. But on my death bed, I will know that my time—all of it: the seconds, and minutes, and hours—they were not wasted. I lived hard, I loved harder; I believed in me when no one else did. I forgave the unforgivable and mostly, I never gave up. I see the fire in you... Remember the warmth of its flames in cold darkness and it will lead you out. I will always be there for you, my angel.

I press the letter to my chest, my heartbeat replying that it has heard the message. I put it carefully into the box with the remaining belongings and proceed more slowly so as not to lose my grip on this precious container.

I head out of the apartment and get startled when the elevator doors open up in front of me before I press the button. I remember that I left the umbrella behind, but decide to not go back for it and step into the elevator.

Leo is standing by the car, awaiting my return. He was able to find a parking spot where his mechanical beast is squeezed between tightly packed vehicles. Rare, large drops of rain start to fall from the sky as the clouds get even darker. I keep my head down and walk fast towards the street crossing, avoiding others who race for cover ahead of the rain. Leo gives me a big wave before I cross the road. The light turns green for me, the car in the next lane over stops and I confidently step on the road. My smile grows wider from the anticipation of spending a night with Leo, the man who turned my love gene on.

The screeching of the brakes and the smell of burned rubber and gasoline reach me before I get to see where it is coming from. Leo's wide smile changes to a look of helpless horror. I catch a glimpse of a wide-eyed driver, tensed up behind the wheel of a white van that just made the corner, but he can't stop in time. It hits me and I am thrown against the hard pavement, hitting my head.

"Someone call an ambulance!" In the dark, I hear Leo barking orders. I can't open my eyes for what seems like minutes. They finally submit to my brain signals and I can see my surroundings, but I am still confused about what happened. My chest feels heavy and my breaths cause me to wince in pain. My head is throbbing with a dull ache; I feel the salty taste of blood in my mouth. I can see Leo's face leaning close to mine. For some reason, I find it funny that he is caring for me as if I am really hurt. I try to raise myself up on my elbows and smile at him. I want to reassure him that I am OK, that I have something exciting to tell him, but my brain shuts my body down and I again collapse into darkness. I can still hear the echo of Leo's voice, "breathing...lucid interval...subdural hematoma... please..." but it gets quieter and quieter before disappearing completely. This time I can't open my eyes as the darkness grows thicker, overpowering me with fear. I think I am really hurt.

"What are you doing here, child?" a familiar voice says softly to me as my feet are being stroked by warm water on a pebbled beach.

I look to the horizon, feeling a deep sensation of loss. I need to be beyond that horizon, but for some reason, I am not in control of my body and I cannot move. Tears run freely down my cheeks, mourning the loss of hope of reaching beyond the visible border in front of me.

I look back and see my grandmother. She is a young woman with long, fiery red hair just like mine, looking at the same horizon as me, but her face expresses complete content. She knows she is where she is supposed to be. She waves and floats closer to me to embrace me in a hug.

"I found Jacob," I tell her, breathing in a comforting smell of rosewater.

"I know, my angel. You have found what I have lost and I gave you what you were not looking for, but you cannot stay here and wait; you have to go back." The riddle doesn't make sense to me.

"But we are surrounded by water - there is nowhere to go." I state the fact that we are isolated on this stone-covered beach.

"I love you, Mila. You have to fight the darkness." She pushes me away with inhuman-like strength and my body is thrown into the waves that pull me under despite my struggling for a breath of air. I feel the cold of the water all around me; I sink deeper, and the darkness envelops me. I keep fighting, just as my grandmother told me. I feel the water entering my lungs and I am gasping for air but all I feel is the pain and the cold of the water in my chest, compressing my body. In a last push of resistance, I look up to the reflective roof of the water, up high. I see the round circle of the sun that glistens amber, sending its rays to me. I reach out, and the invisible force carries me forward to the light of the warm surface.

I open my eyes in a familiar setting of a hospital room, but in an unfamiliar position. I am a patient and I see countless eyes looking at me with expectation.

"Dr. Roth, I am Dr. Kleyn. You are in ICU and I just took a NG tube out. You might feel a burning sensation in your throat. You are in a stable condition. You suffered some injuries in the accident, but I believe you will make a full recovery. I will let you speak to your friends and family—they are anxious to hear from you. If you have any questions, just let me know." An ICU attending with a Tom Selleck mustache and kind blue eyes pauses, and when I thank him, he nods and leaves the room so that he can attend to his other duties. The sweet smell of the ICU is evident here. I know now it is the smell of life and death forces that battle for their victims and survivors in every ICU. Today, I am the lucky one to make it: the sweet smell is the scent of a chance given to live again. I take it in, but wince from the pain. A chest tube penetrates my thoracic cavity, feeding across the bed rail into the pleurovac, a pump which is re-inflating my collapsed lung.

Leo is sitting on the edge of my hospital bed. He looks tired and disheveled. His usually well-trimmed beard seems to have grown and his clothes are all wrinkled; he must have been by my side for quite a while. My mom and dad are standing over me, holding each other up, their faces overshadowed by concern and helplessness. Michelle is holding onto the footboard of my bed, her knuckles protruding through her beautiful, smooth, brown skin. She tries to smile, but she cannot hold it for long and she turns her lips in and looks away, wiping her tears before they become obvious to everyone in the room. I take a deep breath, filling my lungs with air, my chest feels sore and heavy, and I have a burning sensation in my throat, just like Dr. Kleyn told me I would. My head is like a leaded ball, heavy and slow to process what has happened. My left leg feels heavy under the warming blanket. A fluid IV is feeding into my hand, and a foley catheter is taking my urine output. I try to lift myself up, but the gasp from everyone in the room persuades me to stay still. Three 'get well' balloons bop cheerfully from my bed rail, ignoring the solemn atmosphere in the room.

"Hi! How long have I been out?"

"Five days," Leo says, his voice raspy and shaking. I look at my parents to see if what I am hearing is correct. My mother nods, sobbing into my dad's chest.

"You were in a car accident, honey. Thank God Leo was there and had his bag of supplies. You lost consciousness and stopped breathing; he intubated you before paramedics even got to you. You have a few broken ribs—one punctured your lung. Your left femur has a hairline fracture, and you have quite a few bruises and a concussion. But this will heal…" my dad wants to say more, but he is overcome by sobbing that he tries to cover up with his hand. He looks old, not like the man that gives me the bear hugs I am used to. I process the injuries, knowing all too well the healing that will need to happen before I am able to return to full functioning. I don't yet know what it will mean for my residency; I cannot think about it just yet.

"Do you remember anything, Mila?" Leo looks up at me with concern in his eyes; his hand reaches for mine and clasps it gently.

"I don't remember the accident, but I do remember that I wanted to show you something." I search in the depths of my clouded memory for something that I knew before, but now is obscured by my trauma.

"Is this what you wanted to show me?" Leo picks up my grandmother's box and pulls out two pictures of my young grandmother and Jacob.

"Your grandfather…His name is Jacob." I point to the picture of a dashing young man in uniform. Now that Leo is holding up his picture I see an uncanny resemblance: the sharp jaw, the sandy hair, and the eyes of amber. They glow warmly, looking back at me. I bathe in the rays of the gaze, knowing that I found what I was not looking for.

ACKNOWLEDGMENTS

Never would I have imagined that I would write a novel. I am an accidental author. For me, the book writing process was exciting, eye opening, and at times, frustrating. Some weeks I would write every day, and then there was almost a year and a half when I didn't write a single word.

I would like to thank my husband, Michael, for telling me to keep writing and inquiring about the progress of my book. I admire your strength, intelligence, righteousness, and vulnerability. Thank you for giving me your support and unconditional love on daily basis.

My next thank you goes out to Eva Lesko Natiello, the self-published author of The Memory Box and the creator of such workshops as "Book Marketing for Authors" and "Self-Publish Like a Pro." Your story gave me a clear vision of the path for my book. Before taking your workshop, my manuscript had been lying untouched, with just 30,000 words. Two months later, I had over 50,000 words and a complete story.

To my editor, Michael Pilgrim—thank you for all your suggestions and organized approach to my writing. I am grateful for your help with polishing the story so that it is presented to the reader in the best way possible.

Polina Harris, my cousin-in-law, thank you for being my first reader. I am grateful for the time you took to read

Eyes of Amber when it was in its early stages, and then giving me feedback once it was finished.

I would like to thank my Creative Writing professor at Nassau Community College, Robert DiChiara. I enjoyed your class immensely and have the best of memories. The skills you taught me certainly came in handy during the writing of this novel.

I would like to thank my grandparents, especially my Grandmother Olga, and Grandmother Ludmila. I envy your strength of spirit. You survived unbelievable life circumstances at the time of WWII and after it, and are my true inspiration. I will forever treasure the memories of your love.

To my children, thank you for teaching me how to be a better person, how to be inquisitive, and how to enjoy the small moments.

A special thank you goes out to Ebook Launch for creating this book cover, proofreading, as well as the interior design.

BOOK CLUB DISCUSSION QUESTIONS

1. What was the most memorable part of the book?

2. What did you like least about this book?

3. If you were making a movie based on this book, who would you cast?

4. If you got the chance to ask the author of this book one question, what would it be?

5. What do you think the author's purpose was in writing this book? What ideas was she trying to get across?

6. What was your favorite quote?

7. Which character did you relate to the most, and what was it about them that you connected with?

8. What are you having the most trouble imagining and can't wrap your head around?

9. Pretend you are the author's editor. What notes would you give her?

10. Did you learn something from this book that you didn't know before?

11. Do you have an interesting medical encounter of your own?